Topics from the Restless

BOOK ONE

Selections That Intrigue Developing Readers

Third Edition

 JAMESTOWN PUBLISHER

a division of NTC/CONTEMPORARY PUBLISHING GR
Lincolnwood, Illinois USA

Cover Illustration: "The Faces Looking at Each Other" by artist Ricardo Manuel Diaz

ISBN: 0-89061-116-5

Published by Jamestown Publishers,
a division of NTC/Contemporary Publishing Group, Inc.,
4255 West Touhy Avenue,
Lincolnwood (Chicago), Illinois 60712-1975 U.S.A.

3 4 5 6 7 8 9 10 11 12 13 14 15 021 09 08 07 06 05 04 03 02 01

ACKNOWLEDGMENTS

Acknowledgment is gratefully made to the following publishers, authors, and agents for permission to reprint these works. Every effort has been made to determine copyright owners. In the case of any omissions, the Publisher will be pleased to make suitable acknowledgments in future editions.

"Spyglass." From *Mama Makes Up Her Mind* by Bailey White. © 1993 by Bailey White. Reprinted by permission of Addison Wesley Longman.

"The Rake." From *The Cabin: Reminiscence and Diversions* by David Mamet. Copyright © 1992 by David Mamet. Used by permission of Turtle Bay Books, a division of Random House, Inc.

"Borderline." From *Sister to Sister*, edited by Patricia Foster. Copyright © 1995 by Patricia Foster. Used by permission of Doubleday, a division of Bantam Doubleday Dell Publishing Group, Inc.

"Becoming Number One," adapted from Chapter 6 of *Volunteer Slavery: My Authentic Negro Experience* by Jill Nelson. Copyright © 1993 by Jill Nelson, published by The Noble Press, Inc., Chicago.

"How We Kept Mother's Day." From *Laugh with Leacock* by Stephen Leacock. Copyright © 1930 by Dodd, Mead & Company, Inc. Copyright renewed 1958 by George Leacock.

"Cajun Country." Reprinted by permission of The Putnam Publishing Group from *Charles Kuralt's America* by Charles Kuralt. Copyright © 1995 by Charles Kuralt.

"Into the Kenyan Game Reserve." Extract reproduced from *Pole to Pole with Michael Palin* by Michael Palin with permission of BBC Worldwide Limited.

Excerpt from "In Its Decay, Butte Sees a National Treasure" by Timothy Egan. From *The New York Times*, August 30, 1997. Copyright © 1997 by The New York Times Company. Reprinted by permission.

"Letter from France: From Berkeley to James Baldwin and Back" by Maya Angelou. Appeared in *Holiday* magazine, March 1974. Reprinted by permission of The Helen Brann Agency, Inc.

"Moscow on the Make" by Bill Powell and Owen Matthews. From *Newsweek*, September 1, 1997. © 1997, Newsweek, Inc. All rights reserved. Reprinted by permission.

Excerpt from "Red Fire Farm" by Anchee Min. Reprinted with permission from *Granta*. Copyright © 1992, Anchee Min.

"The Cow-Tail Switch." From *The Cow-Tail Switch and Other West African Stories* by Harold Courlander and George Herzog, Copyright 1947, © 1974 by George Herzog. Reprinted by permission of Henry Holt and Company, Inc.

"Then Came the Famous *Kristallnacht*" by Elise Radell as told to Joan Morrison and Charlotte Fox Zabusky. Copyright © 1980 by Joan Morrison and Charlotte Fox Zabusky in *American Mosaic*. Currently available in paperback from the University of Pittsburgh Press.

"Children of the A-Bomb." Reprinted by permission of The Putnam Publishing Group from *Children of the A-Bomb* by Atsuko Tsujioka as told to Dr. Arata Osada. Copyright © 1959 by Dr. Arata Osada.

"After Twenty Years" From *After Twenty Years* by O. Henry.

"The Day I Nearly Drowned" by June Mellies Reno. Copyright © 1974 by the Hearst Corporation. Originally appeared in *Good Housekeeping*. Reprinted by permission of the author and the author's agents, Scott Meredith Literary Agency, L.P.

"Autumn Storm." From *The Wildlife Stories of Faith McNulty* by Faith McNulty. Copyright © 1980 by Faith McNulty.

"Into Thin Air." From *Into Thin Air* by Jon Krakauer. Copyright © 1997 by Jon Krakauer. Reprinted by permission of Random House, Inc.

"A Match to the Heart." From *A Match to the Heart* by Gretel Ehrlich. Copyright © 1994 by Gretel Ehrlich. Reprinted by permission of Pantheon Books, a division of Random House, Inc.

"Alive." From *Alive: The Story of the Andes Survivors* by Piers Paul Read. Copyright © 1974 by Piers Paul Read. Reprinted by permission of HarperCollins Publishers, Inc.

Photographs
Page 7: David Hanover/Tony Stone Images.
Page 10: The Image Bank/Grant V. Faint.
Page 15: Tony Stone Images/Shaun Egan.
Page 21: The Image Bank/H. De Lespinasse.
Page 27: The Stock Market/Jose L. Pelaez, Inc.
Page 33: The Image Bank/Petrified Collection.
Page 39: Charles Thatcher/Tony Stone Images.
Page 42: National Geographic/Jonathan Blair.
Page 48: The Stock Market/Harvey Lloyd.
Page 53: Patrick Krohn/NYT Pictures.
Page 59: The Image Bank/Hans Wolf.
Page 65: © Tony Stone Images/Steven Weinberg.
Page 71: Tony Stone Images/Hulton Getty.
Page 74: UPI/Corbis-Bettmann.
Page 80: National Geographic/Robert W. Moore.
Page 85: UPI/Corbis-Bettmann.
Page 91: UPI/Corbis-Bettmann.
Page 97: The Image Bank/Petrified Collection.
Page 103: Peter Rauter/Tony Stone Images.
Page 106: The Image Bank/Robert Farber.
Page 112: The Image Bank/Patti McConville.
Page 118: National Geographic/Barry Bishop.
Page 124: The Image Bank/Lionel F. Brown.
Page 130: © Tony Stone Images/John Warden.

CONTENTS

TOPIC 4: FACING THE ELEMENTS — 103

Introductory Selection

READING PURPOSE—
The following passage will tell you about the selections in this book and how they are structured. As you read, decide which selection part will help you improve your reading most. (After you have completed the vocabulary activity and before you begin reading, turn to page 4 and record the hours and minutes in the box labeled *Starting Time*.)

VOCABULARY—PART ONE

All of these words are in the selection you are about to read. Study each word and its meaning. Then answer the questions below. As you read the selection, notice how each vocabulary word is used.

intent: purpose

aspects: parts; features; elements

oppression: persecution; great hardship

compelling: very interesting or attention-getting

slant: angle; viewpoint

efficient: performing a task easily and skillfully

consecutively: coming one after another in order

corresponding: matching

diagnostic: helping to analyze or find problems in

discriminating: able to see differences and distinctions

---

1. Which word could describe a person who works without wasting any effort?

2. Which word would describe a person who could easily tell the difference between real and fake emeralds?

3. Which word could describe a movie that held your interest so strongly you could hardly stand for it to end?

4. If you counted from 1 to 100 in order, how would you be presenting the numbers?

5. Which word would you use if you were describing a test that told you about your reading strengths and weaknesses?

(Enter your starting time on page 4 now.)

1   You are using this text for two purposes: (1) to improve your reading and study skills and (2) to read stories and articles about topics that will both interest you and make you think.

2   The topics and selections in these books span the range of human experience. The editors' intent in choosing them was to show aspects of the real world, but another, equally important, purpose was to present materials simply because they are interesting. Serious or amusing, the topics in these books will help you get involved with the reality of today's world.

3   The other purpose for using this series, that of reading and study improvement, recognizes another kind of reality. The series will help you to develop skills and techniques necessary for success.

4   In the books in *Topics from the Restless* you will read not only about serious matters like preserving the environment, knowing the dangers of alcohol and other drugs, and recognizing injustice and oppression. You will also find less serious stories and articles about interesting ways that people make a living, fascinating cities and regions around the world, and thrilling encounters with disaster. Though you may not find each selection equally compelling, there are enough choices to get you interested in reading and to show you how exciting stories in books, newspapers, and magazines can be.

5   Each book in this series is divided into units of five reading selections. These selections will cover different aspects of the unit topic, or perhaps present different opinions on that topic. Sometimes one selection in the unit will be a bit more difficult than the others, and sometimes you will see how a writer of fiction can give a new and different slant to a topic. By the time you have finished reading the selections in a unit, you should be something of an expert on the topic. At the very least, you will be familiar with various ways to look at it.

6   Included with each selection is a study skills exercise. In these exercises, you will learn methods of understanding, critical thinking skills, techniques of comprehension, and many other key ways to improve your reading ability. The study skills exercises are designed to help you develop efficient reading techniques. As you read the selections in this book, you will find that often one study skills exercise leads to the next. It is important to read

and work the study skills exercises consecutively to understand each subject fully. You will come to see that each kind of reading matter demands a corresponding reading technique.

Using the Topics

7   The 20 selections following this introductory one are designed to be read in numerical order, starting with Selection 1 and ending with Selection 20. Because the selections generally increase in difficulty as you progress through the book, the earlier ones may prepare you to handle the upcoming ones successfully.

8   Here are the procedures to follow for reading each selection:

9   **1. Answer the Vocabulary Questions.** At the beginning of each lesson, immediately preceding the selection, is a vocabulary-previewing activity. The activity includes 10 vocabulary words from the selection, their meanings as they are used in the selection, and 5 questions related to those words. To answer each question, you will choose from and write one of the 10 vocabulary words. Previewing the vocabulary in this way will give you a head start on understanding the words when you encounter them in the selection. In the selection itself the words are underlined for easy reference.

10   **2. Preview Before Reading.** Previewing acquaints you with the overall content and structure of the selection before you actually read. It is like consulting a road map before taking a trip: planning the route gives you more confidence as you proceed and, perhaps, helps you avoid any unnecessary delays. Previewing should take about a minute or two and is done in this way:

11   a) Read the title. Learn the writer's subject and, possibly, his or her point of view on it.

12   b) Read the opening and closing paragraphs. These contain the introductory and concluding remarks. Important information is frequently presented in these key paragraphs.

13   c) Skim through. Try to discover the author's approach to the subject. Does he or she use many examples? Is the writer's purpose to convince you about certain ideas? What else can you learn now to help you when you read?

14   **3. Establish a Reading Purpose.** After you have previewed the selection, establish a purpose for reading it. The suggestion that precedes the selection will help you complete the activities.

15 **4. Read the Selection.** Do not try to race through. Read carefully so that you can answer the comprehension questions that follow.

16 · Keep track of your reading time by noting when you start and finish. A table on page 136 converts your reading time to a words-per-minute rate. Select the time from the table that is closest to your reading time. Record those figures in the boxes at the end of the selection. There is no one ideal reading speed for everything. The efficient reader varies reading speed as the selection requires.

17 **5. Answer the Comprehension Questions.** After you have read the selection, find the comprehension questions that follow. These have been included to test your understanding of what you have read. The questions are diagnostic, too. Because the comprehension skill being measured is identified, you can detect your areas of weakness.

18 Read each question carefully and select one of the four choices that answers the question most accurately or most completely. Frequently all four choices, or options, given for a question are correct, but one is the best answer. For this reason some comprehension questions are highly challenging and require you to be highly discriminating. You may, from time to time, disagree with an answer. When this happens, you can sharpen your powers of discrimination. Study the question again and seek to discover why the listed answer may be best. When you disagree with the text, you are thinking. When you objectively analyze and recognize your errors, you are learning.

19 A profitable habit for you to acquire is analyzing the questions you have answered incorrectly. If time permits, return to the selection to find and underline the passages containing the correct answers. This helps you see what you missed the first time. Some interpretive and generalizing questions are not answered specifically in the text. In these cases, bracket the part of the selection that refers to the correct answer.

20 **6. Answer Additional Vocabulary Questions.** Following the comprehension section are two sets of sentences using the 10 vocabulary words introduced earlier. Each fill-in-the-blank sentence requires you to choose the correct word by looking at the context (surrounding words). This format helps you improve your ability to use context to understand words. The efficient use of context is a valuable vocabulary tool.

21 The boxes following the vocabulary activity contain space for your comprehension score and your vocabulary score. Each correct vocabulary item is worth 10 points, and each correct comprehension answer is worth 10 points.

22 A profitable habit for you to acquire is analyzing the questions you have answered incorrectly. If time permits, return to the selection to find and underline the passages containing the correct answers. This helps you see what you missed the first time. Some interpretive and generalizing questions are not answered specifically in the text. In these cases, bracket the part of the selection that refers to the correct answer.

23 Pages 137 and 138 contain graphs to be used for plotting your scores and tallying your incorrect responses. On page 137 record your comprehension score at the appropriate intersection of lines, using an X. Use a circle on the same graph to record your vocabulary results. Some students prefer to use different color inks, or pencil and ink, to distinguish between comprehension and vocabulary plottings.

24 On page 138 darken the squares to indicate the comprehension questions you have missed. By referring to the Skills Profile as you progress through the text, you and your instructor will be able to tell which questions give you the most trouble. As soon as you detect a specific weakness in comprehension, consult your instructor to see what supplementary materials he or she can provide or suggest.

25 **7. Write About the Selection.** A brief writing activity allows you to offer your own opinions about some aspect of the selection. Here you are always asked to respond briefly, which means you do not have to go on for pages. A clearly written paragraph or two, using as many specific facts or examples as possible, is enough to complete each writing assignment.

26 **8. Complete the Study Skills Exercises.** Concluding each lesson is a passage on study skills followed by five completion questions to be answered after you have finished the passage. One or two of these questions will always ask you to apply the study skill to the selection you have just read.

Using the Topic Review

27 At the end of each unit of selections is a Topic Review consisting of six questions. These questions deal with the unit as a whole and so may

3

ask you to think about the selections in new ways, such as by comparing and contrasting them or by making generalizations about their content. One question will always require you to apply a study skill from the unit to one or more of the selections.

28   The questions in the Topic Review are designed to be answered in writing. Your instructor, however, may choose to have you discuss some or all of them in class. He or she may also suggest that you answer only certain questions or may have you pick a certain number of them to answer.

29   Each lesson and each Topic Review is set up in the manner just described. When you have finished doing the activities in this introductory material, go on to the first selection for Topic 1.

Starting Time	
Finishing Time	
Reading Time	
Reading Rate	

COMPREHENSION

Read the following questions and statements. For each one, put an X in the box before the option that contains the most complete or accurate answer.

1. How much time should be spent on previewing?
   - ☐ a. Your time will vary with each selection.
   - ☐ b. Previewing should take one or two minutes.
   - ☐ c. No specific time is suggested.
   - ☐ d. None—the instructor times the selection.

2. The way the vocabulary exercises are described suggests that
   - ☐ a. the meaning of a word often depends on how the word is used in the selection.
   - ☐ b. the final authority for word meaning is the dictionary.
   - ☐ c. words have precise and permanent meanings.
   - ☐ d. certain words are always difficult to understand.

3. The writer of this passage presents the facts in order of
   - ☐ a. importance.   ☐ c. time.
   - ☐ b. purpose.   ☐ d. operation.

4. *Topics from the Restless* is based on which of the following premises?
   - ☐ a. Students should know about today's world.
   - ☐ b. Students learn best from reading newspapers and magazines.
   - ☐ c. The only worthwhile articles are long and serious.
   - ☐ d. Traditional reading improvement texts rarely accomplish their purpose.

5. How does the writer feel about reading speed?
   - ☐ a. It is a minimal aspect of the total reading situation.
   - ☐ b. It is second (following comprehension) in the ranking of skills.
   - ☐ c. It is connected to comprehension.
   - ☐ d. It should be developed at an early age.

6. The introductory selection
   - ☐ a. eliminates the need for oral instruction.
   - ☐ b. explains the proper use of the text in detail.
   - ☐ c. permits the student to learn by doing.
   - ☐ d. allows for variety and interest.

7. The introductory selection suggests that
   - ☐ a. most readers are not flexible.
   - ☐ b. students should learn to use different reading skills for different types of reading matter.
   - ☐ c. students today read better than students of the past did.
   - ☐ d. 20 selections is an ideal number for a reading improvement text.

8. The overall tone of this passage is
   - ☐ a. serious.   ☐ c. humorous.
   - ☐ b. suspenseful.   ☐ d. sarcastic.

9. The author of this selection is probably
   - ☐ a. a doctor.   ☐ c. an educator.
   - ☐ b. an accountant.   ☐ d. a businessman.

10. The writer of this passage makes his or her point clear by
   - ☐ a. telling a story.
   - ☐ b. listing historical facts.
   - ☐ c. using metaphors.
   - ☐ d. giving directions.

Comprehension Skills Key

1. recalling specific facts
2. retaining concepts
3. organizing facts
4. understanding the main idea
5. drawing a conclusion
6. making a judgment
7. making an inference
8. recognizing tone
9. understanding characters
10. appreciating literary forms

VOCABULARY—PART TWO

Write the word that makes the most sense in each sentence.

aspects	efficient
intent	consecutively
oppression	

1. The purpose of this series was not to make reading dull and boring; instead, its _____ was to show how interesting reading can be.

2. The selections deal with amusing topics as well as serious ones, such as injustice and other forms of _____ .

3. Many _____ of each topic are presented, so the reader can have contact with a wide range of viewpoints about that topic.

4. Because the study skills are presented in order, it is important to study each lesson _____ .

5. Learning to apply the study skills as you go through this book will make you a more _____ reader.

diagnostic	discriminating
corresponding	compelling
slant	

6. Though a few selections may bore you, you should find most of them _____ .

7. Most selections were chosen because the writers have a distinct point of view and an interesting _____ on their topics.

8. When answering the comprehension questions following a selection, you should mark the blank _____ to the right response.

9. Some of the questions are difficult and require you to be _____ between the possible answers.

10. You can use your wrong answers in a _____ way to figure out your reading weaknesses.

Comprehension [ ]

Vocabulary [ ]

UNDERSTANDING THROUGH WRITING

Think about the weaknesses you might have as a reader. In what ways do you think the selections in this book will be most helpful in overcoming them? Write a paragraph explaining what you think. Be as specific as you can.

_____

_____

_____

_____

_____

_____

_____

_____

BUILDING STUDY SKILLS

Read the following passage and answer the questions that follow it.

Why Learn Study Skills?

You may wonder why you still need to learn how to study at this point in your life. You may feel you know all there is to know about studying.

But do you really? Have you ever found yourself in the same situation as these people?

• A student quickly reads the directions to his friend's house and thinks he knows where he's going. But he gets lost on the way.

• A woman needs to find one small fact in an 800-page biography. After 45 minutes, she has looked through the first 250 pages and still has not found what she wanted.

• A businessman enjoys reading fiction and can get through a mystery novel in two nights. But when he reads documents at work, he has trouble understanding them.

Maybe you recognized the problem each of these people had. The student could have jotted down notes or drawn a rough map to help himself remember the directions. The woman could have found the information she needed by using the book's index. The businessman should have slowed down when he read more difficult materials, such as business documents.

It is clear that study skills are skills that can help you far beyond the classroom. Whenever you have to read, locate, or understand information, your job will be easier if you call on the appropriate study skill.

Today's reader must be flexible enough to choose the skills that suit each reading task. As you complete the selections and exercises in this book, you will find yourself improving your reading technique. The more techniques you master, the easier you will make your life in school, as well as in the outside world.

1. You may feel you know a lot about

_____ already.

2. You may remember that to find information in a book, you can use the book's

_____ .

3. Study skills can help you whenever you have to read, locate, or _____ information.

4. Today's reader must be _____ enough to choose a suitable skill for each reading task.

5. The selections and exercises in this book will help you grow in _____ .

To lose one parent may be regarded as a misfortune; to lose both looks like carelessness.

—Oscar Wilde (1854–1900)

FAMILY PORTRAITS

Spyglass

Bailey White

R E A D I N G   P U R P O S E —
This selection shows how a gift given to one family member can change that person's life. Read to find out what the gift was, who received it, and what effects it had.

VOCABULARY—PART ONE

All of these words are in the selection you are about to read. Study each word and its meaning. Then answer the questions below. As you read the selection, notice how each vocabulary word is used.

unruly: wild; difficult to control

celestial: having to do with the sky

whim: sudden impulse or urge

virulent: very harmful; deadly

impervious: resistant

mobility: ability to move around

incensed: very angry

premium: prize; reward

disarray: disorder

marine: having to do with the sea

---

1. Which word could describe a flu epidemic so serious that it has killed several elderly people?

2. Which word could describe the condition of a room with books, papers, and clothes thrown everywhere?

3. Which word might a mother use to describe her children when they run around wild and refuse to listen to her?

4. Which word names an advantage a person gets when he or she buys a car for the first time?

5. Which word might describe a decision you make without planning or any advance thought?

1   My father craved an adventurous life, and when I was just a little girl, he went off with an anthropological[1] team from the Field Museum of Natural History to study and record the physical characteristics of four fierce groups of people in southwestern Asia. My father had no training as an anthropometrist, and his job on the expedition, as close as we could figure it, was to grab the subjects and hold them still while the scientists applied the spreading calipers[2] and the anthropometer, and took hair and blood samples "where possible."

2   The leader of the expedition, a famous physical anthropologist, was a kind gentleman, and he took pity on my mother, who was to be left at home for a year and a half with a farm to run and three unruly children, and he gave her, as a parting gift, his telescope. It was a beautiful instrument, all gleaming brass and leather and ebony, with a wonderfully silent sliding action and a muffled *thunk* as at achieved its full-open position. On the day they left, Professor Meade laid it in my mother's hands. "My great-grandfather had it at Trafalgar," he told her. "Now I want you to have it." Then he said good-bye and swept away, leaving us in a swirl of English pipe tobacco, old leather, and oiled canvas, my father staggering along behind him, dragging the cases of clattering instruments.

3   The year and a half went by, and my mother studied every distant object she could find, from celestial bodies in the night sky to the pond a mile away from our house, which through the lenses of Professor Meade's telescope looked like a bright, magical place where frogs leapt silently and deer drinking at the water's edge had no fear of people.

4   My father came back, sunburned and irritable. He had presents for us: for my brother, a Persian dagger with a jeweled handle; for my mother, a lamp made out of the bladders of two camels; and for my sister and me, exquisite rag dolls that had little hands with separated fingers like real hands, and ferocious embroidered faces with furious dark eyes and sullen red satin-stitched lips.

5   My brother developed amazing skills with the dagger and terrorized the neighborhood with feats of knife throwing, and my mother, on a creative whim, turned the camel-bladder lamp upside down and hung it by an electrical cord over the dining-room table. She wouldn't let us play with the dolls.

She suspected lice and packed them away in moth-balls. My father himself had a serious infestation of crabs—some virulent southwestern Asian strain impervious to the pediculicides[3] of the New World.

6   Soon my father went off on another adventure, but this time he never came back. The camel-bladder chandelier could not seem to adjust to the climate of south Georgia: in the summer it would droop and swag and stretch in the damp heat until it almost touched the tabletop, and in the winter it would shrink and suck itself into a tight snarl up near the ceiling.

7   The years went by. My mother got old and crippled. And as her mobility decreased, she grew more and more dependent on Professor Meade's telescope. "Bring me my spyglass!" she would call. Someone would fetch it, she would put her elbows on the windowsill, lean the shaft of the telescope against the frame, and gaze.

8   Then one day we got a telephone call from a granddaughter of Professor Meade's. She wanted to see us "on a matter of some importance," she said. She flew down from Chicago. Professor Meade was on his deathbed. He was dying peacefully. There was only one thing he wanted: his grandfather's telescope.

9   My brother was incensed. He had recently taken the telescope apart into its thousand pieces to clean the lenses and change the felts. It had taken him two weeks. "What does a dying man need with a telescope?" he fumed.

10   My sister and I asked, "Now what will Mama look at things through?"

11   But it didn't bother Mama one bit. "His great-grandfather had it at Trafalgar," she said. "Of course he shall have it back." And she carefully slid the telescope into its Morocco leather case, snapped the snaps, and gave it to Professor Meade's granddaughter.

12   And Mama didn't seem to miss it. As a premium in the thirty-dollar pledge category for the local public radio station she got a pair of tiny plastic binoculars. Looking through those binoculars was the equivalent of taking three steps closer to your subject. "But it's hard for me to take three steps," she pointed out, the binoculars clamped to her eyes. She used to be able to sweep the telescope into position, with the near distance, middle distance, and remote distance swirling and colliding in brilliant,

---

[1]*anthropological:* related to the study of peoples' cultures and beliefs
[2]*calipers:* instruments used to measure the thickness of something

[3]*pediculicides:* substances that kill lice

sharp <u>disarray</u>, and then focus on an osprey catching a fish a mile away, a silent explosion of bright water. Now, with the binoculars, she could see the purple finches on the bird feeder at the kitchen window a bit clearer, and recognize friends and family members when they came to call a moment before they opened the screen door, stepped inside, and said to her, "Put those damned binoculars down, Lila."

"My mother studied every distant object she could find, from celestial bodies in the night sky to the pond a mile away from our house."

13 One summer we made a family trek to a wild island off the coast of north Florida. We stayed in a house with a big screen porch on the bay side. It was hard for Mama to walk on the soft sand, so she sat on the porch all day, staring through her binoculars out over the marsh.

14 Every morning a boat from the local <u>marine</u> lab would pull up and anchor just off shore. People would wade around in the marsh grass with nets and spades and bottles. By the end of the first week the screen was bulged out from the pressure of Mama's binoculars. She didn't seem to understand that they did not give her the same dignity of distance she had been able to achieve with the telescope. We tried to reason with her. "They can see you, Mama," we hissed. But she just pressed the binoculars harder against the screen.

15 "What are they doing? What are they doing down there?" she asked.

16 Then one evening a man came up to the house. We recognized him from the morning marine lab group. "Oh no," we thought.

17 "Where is that old woman with the little tiny binoculars?" he asked. We shuffled around and shuffled around. Someone went and got her from in the house.

18 He shook her hand. "My name is Lewis," he said, "Walter Lewis. Would you like to see what we're doing down there?" And very carefully he helped her over the sand to the marsh.

19 For the rest of our stay on the island, Mama would make her way down the beach every morning. She would sit in a chair at the water's edge and look at the things they brought up.

20 "It's clams," she told us. "They're studying a certain kind of clam." Dr. Lewis gave her books, and she sat up all night reading about bivalve mollusks.

21 At the end of our last week on the island Dr. Lewis came up to the house to say good-bye. "A group of us from the marine lab are leaving this afternoon to do a little more work on the migration of the spiny lobster," he said to Mama. "We thought you might like to come along."

22 The last we saw of Mama that summer, she was heading for the open ocean. We stood on the dock and waved good-bye. But she didn't see us. She was leaning forward in the bow of the boat with her little plastic binoculars pressed to her eyes, peering out to sea.

Starting Time	
Finishing Time	
Reading Time	
Reading Rate	

COMPREHENSION

Read the following questions and statements. For each one, put an X in the box before the option that contains the most complete or accurate answer.

1. The telescope was originally given as a gift to
   ☐ a. the author.
   ☐ b. the author's mother.
   ☐ c. the author's father.
   ☐ d. the author's brother.

2. The events in this story take place
   - ☐ a. in one place and in the period of a month.
   - ☐ b. in one place and over several years.
   - ☐ c. in two places and over several years.
   - ☐ d. in two places and over the period of a month.

3. The details in this story are presented
   - ☐ a. in time order.
   - ☐ b. in spatial order.
   - ☐ c. by moving back and forth between present and past.
   - ☐ d. in order of importance.

4. Another good title for this story would be
   - ☐ a. How Mama Got Along Without a Husband.
   - ☐ b. From a Telescope to Binoculars.
   - ☐ c. Gifts from an Absent Father.
   - ☐ d. Seeing the World Through Mama's Eyes.

5. Mama doesn't mind returning the telescope because
   - ☐ a. she is tired of using it.
   - ☐ b. Professor Meade has been a close friend of hers.
   - ☐ c. she understands its value to Professor Meade.
   - ☐ d. she wants to teach her children not to be selfish.

6. Dr. Lewis asks Mama to join his expedition because
   - ☐ a. he is romantically interested in her.
   - ☐ b. he appreciates her interest in his project.
   - ☐ c. he pities her because she is an old woman.
   - ☐ d. his co-workers have asked him to.

7. The binoculars and the telescope are valuable to Mama because they
   - ☐ a. help her stay in touch with the world.
   - ☐ b. provide a way of snooping on other people.
   - ☐ c. make up for her poor eyesight.
   - ☐ d. let her rely less on her children.

8. The overall tone of this selection is
   - ☐ a. sad.
   - ☐ b. serious.
   - ☐ c. lighthearted.
   - ☐ d. angry.

9. Mama can best be characterized as

   - ☐ a. a fairly serious scientist.
   - ☐ b. a mother with little concern for her children.
   - ☐ c. a woman with a desire to be a world traveler.
   - ☐ d. a woman who refuses to let age slow her down.

10. This story is told by a
   - ☐ a. first-person narrator.
   - ☐ b. second-person narrator.
   - ☐ c. third-person limited narrator.
   - ☐ d. third-person omniscient narrator.

Comprehension Skills Key

1. recalling specific facts	6. making a judgment
2. retaining concepts	7. making an inference
3. organizing facts	8. recognizing tone
4. understanding the main idea	9. understanding characters
5. drawing a conclusion	10. appreciating literary forms

VOCABULARY—PART TWO

Write the word that makes the most sense in each sentence.

celestial	**impervious**
mobility	**disarray**
marine	

1. Mama's _____ decreased as she got older; she found it harder and harder to get around.

2. The telescope helped her get good views of the moon and other _____ bodies.

3. Later, she became interested in clams and other _____ creatures.

4. Mama's house got untidy and the rooms were in _____ , but she didn't worry about straightening things up.

5. Friends tried to warn Mama about the effects of untidiness, but she was _____ to criticism.

11

incensed	unruly
whim	virulent
premium	

6. After their father left, the children were

    _____ and hard to control.

7. The son had a bad temper and became

    _____ when things didn't go his

    way.

8. In fact, the mother offered a

    _____ to any baby-sitter who

    could control him.

9. One of the daughters was very free-spirited and

    often did things on _____ .

10. At one time she caught a _____

    disease because she had visited a country where

    people were dying from it.

Comprehension [ ]

Vocabulary [ ]

UNDERSTANDING
THROUGH WRITING

How did getting the telescope change Mama's life?
Use ideas from the story to write about some of the
ways Mama changed after she received this gift.

_____

_____

_____

_____

_____

_____

_____

BUILDING STUDY SKILLS

Read the following passage and answer the questions that follow it.

Previewing

Students frequently ask, What can I do to improve my reading? Believe it or not, there is a one-word answer to that question: preview.

It is a bad idea to jump into a story or article with the first word and try to meet the author's ideas head-on. This approach is poor because it is inefficient. To be efficient in reading, you must scout the text to see how the author writes. That will help you discover the best way to read the work.

What do you do before assembling a jigsaw puzzle? You probably study the picture to see what the puzzle looks like with the pieces in the proper places. Do that in reading as well. See the whole picture before you begin putting the words and ideas together. See where the author is going, what he or she plans to say, and what concepts or examples will be used to present ideas. If you can discover the author's main point and the arguments supporting it before you begin to read, you can begin to organize and interpret the ideas right away. As a result, you can read intelligently and see how everything fits.

1. _____ to improve your perfor-

    mance when you read.

2. You should see the whole _____

    before you put words and ideas together.

3. If you had looked through this article before you

    began reading it, you would have seen that the

    writer was focusing mostly on events in the life of

    her _____ .

4. You would also have seen that the article was not

    about the writer's _____ , as the

    opening paragraphs seem to suggest.

5. By looking through the text before you read, you

    can begin to _____ and interpret

    the author's ideas right from the start.

2

The Rake

David Mamet

READING PURPOSE—
In this selection the author describes life with his mother, stepfather, and sister. Read to learn his feelings about that life.

VOCABULARY—PART ONE

All of these words are in the story you are about to read. Study each word and its meaning. Then answer the questions below. As you read the story, notice how each vocabulary word is used. You will have more questions about the words later.

adjacent: next to; nearby

proprietary: having to do with ownership

innovations: new ideas or practices

engendered: brought into existence

utopian: like an ideal state or country with perfect laws

signal: remarkable; notable

prospect: something looked forward to

camaraderie: friendship; comradeship

avert: prevent; avoid

proximity: nearness

---

1. Which word might you use in talking about your feelings when you are with a close friend?

   _____

2. Which word could describe a society in which all people were treated fairly and everyone obeyed the laws?

   _____

3. Which word might describe the interest a person takes in a car that belongs to him?

   _____

4. Which word could be a synonym for *expectation*?

   _____

5. Which word could be an antonym for *ordinary*?

   _____

1　There was the incident of the rake and there was the incident of the school play, and it seems to me that they both took place at the round kitchen table.

2　The table was not in the kitchen proper, but in an area called the "nook," which held its claim to that small measure of charm by dint of a waist-high wall separating it from an <u>adjacent</u> area known as the living room.

3　All family meals were eaten in the nook. There was a dining room to the right, but, as in most rooms of that name at that time and in those sur-roundings, it was never used.

4　The round table was of wrought iron and topped with glass; it was noteworthy for that glass, for it was more than once and rather more than several times, I am inclined to think, that my stepfather would grow so angry as to bring some object down on the glass top, shattering it, thus giving us to know how we had forced him out of control.

5　And it seems that most times when he would shatter the table, as often as that might have been, he would cut some portion of himself on the glass, or that he or his wife, our mother, would cut their hands picking up the glass afterward, and that we children were to understand, and did understand, that these wounds were our fault.

6　So the table was associated in our minds with the notion of blood.

7　The house was in a brand-new housing develop-ment in the southern suburbs. The new community was built upon, and now bordered, the remains of what had once been a cornfield. When our new family moved in, there were but a few homes in the development completed, and a few more under construction. Most streets were mud, and boasted a house here or there, and many empty lots marked out by white stakes.

8　The house we lived in was the development's model home. The first time we had seen it, it had signs plastered on the front and throughout the interior telling of the various conveniences it con-tained. And it had a lawn, one of the only homes in the new community that did.

9　My stepfather was fond of the lawn, and he de-tailed me and my sister to care for it, and one fall afternoon we found ourselves assigned to rake the leaves.

10　Why this chore should have been so hated I can-not say, except that we children, and I especially, felt ourselves less than full members of this new, cobbled-together family, and disliked being assigned to the beautification of a home that we found unbeautiful in all respects, and for which we had neither natural affection nor a sense of <u>propri-etary</u> interest.

11　We went to the new high school. We walked the mile down the open two-lane road on one side of which was the just-begun suburban community and on the other side of which was the cornfield.

12　The school was as new as the community, and still under construction for the first three years of its occupancy. One of its <u>innovations</u> was the no-tion that honesty would be <u>engendered</u> by the ab-sence of security, so the lockers were designed and built both without locks and without the possibility of attaching locks. And there was the correspond-ing rash of thievery and many lectures about the same from the school administration, but it was difficult to point with pride to any scholastic or community tradition supporting the suggestion that we, the students, pull together in this new, <u>utopian</u> way. We were in school in an uncompleted build-ing in the midst of a mud field in the midst of a cornfield. Our various sports teams were called the Spartans; and I played on those teams, which were of a wretchedness consistent with their novelty.

13　Meanwhile, my sister interested herself in the drama society. The year after I had left the school she obtained the lead in the school play. It called for acting and singing, both of which she had talent for, and it looked to be a <u>signal</u> triumph for her in her otherwise unremarkable and unenjoyed school career.

14　On the night of the play's opening she sat down to dinner with our mother and our stepfather. It may be that they ate a trifle early to allow her to get to the school to enjoy the excitement of the opening night. But however it was, my sister had no appetite, and she nibbled a bit at her food, and then when she got up from the table to carry her plate back to scrape it in the sink, my mother sug-gested that she sit down, as she had not finished her food. My sister said she really had no appetite, but my mother insisted that, as the meal had been prepared, it would be good form to sit and eat it.

15　My sister sat down with the plate and pecked at her food and she tried to eat a bit, and told my mother that, no, really, she possessed no appetite whatsoever, and that was due, no doubt, not to the food, but to her nervousness and excitement at the <u>prospect</u> of opening night.

16 My mother, again, said that, as the food had been cooked, it had to be eaten, and my sister tried and said that she could not; at which my mother nodded. She then got up from the table and went to the telephone and looked up the number and called the school and got the drama teacher and identified herself and told him that her daughter wouldn't be coming to school that night, that, no, she was not ill, but that she would not be coming in. Yes, yes, she said, she knew that her daughter had the lead in the play, and, yes, she was aware that many children and teachers

"My stepfather was fond of the lawn,…and one fall afternoon we found ourselves assigned to rake the leaves."

had worked hard for it, et cetera; and so my sister did not play the lead in her school play. But I was long gone, out of the house by that time, and well out of it. I heard that story, and others like it, at the distance of twenty-five years.

17 When we left the house we left in good spirits. When we went out to dinner, it was an adventure, which was strange to me, looking back, because many of these dinners ended with my sister or myself being banished, sullen or in tears, from the restaurant, and told to wait in the car, as we were in disgrace.

18 These were the excursions that had ended due to her or my intolerable arrogance, as it was explained to us.

19 The happy trips were celebrated and capped with a joke. Here is the joke: my stepfather, my mother, my sister, and I would exit the restaurant, my stepfather and mother would walk to the car, telling us that they would pick us up. We children would stand by the restaurant entrance. They

would drive up in the car, open the passenger door, and wait until my sister and I had started to get in. They would then drive away.

20 They would drive ten or fifteen feet and open the door again, and we would walk up again, and they would drive away again. They sometimes would drive around the block. But they would always come back, and by that time the four of us would be laughing in camaraderie and appreciation of what, I believe, was our only family joke.

21 We were doing the lawn, my sister and I. I was raking, and she was stuffing the leaves into a bag. I loathed the job, and my muscles and my mind rebelled, and I was viciously angry, and my sister said something, and I turned and threw the rake at her and it hit her in the face.

22 The rake was split bamboo and metal, and a piece of metal caught her lip and cut her badly.

23 We were both terrified, and I was sick with guilt, and we ran into the house, my sister holding her hand to her mouth, and her mouth and her hand and the front of her dress covered in blood.

24 We ran into the kitchen, where my mother was cooking dinner, and my mother asked what happened.

25 Neither of us—myself out of guilt, or course, and my sister out of a desire to avert the terrible punishment she knew I would receive—would say what had occurred.

26 My mother pressed us, and neither of us would answer. She said that until one or the other answered, we would not go to the hospital; and so the family sat down to dinner, where my sister

clutched a napkin to her face and the blood soaked the napkin and ran down onto her food, which she had to eat; and I also ate my food, and we cleared the table and went to the hospital.

27   I remember the walks home from school in the frigid winter, along the cornfield that was, for all its <u>proximity</u> to the city, part of the prairie. The winters were viciously cold. From the remove of years, I can see how the area might and may have been beautiful. One could have walked in the stubble of the cornfields, or hunted birds, or enjoyed any of a number of pleasures naturally occurring.

Starting Time [ ]

Finishing Time [ ]

Reading Time [ ]

Reading Rate [ ]

COMPREHENSION

Read the following questions and statements. For each one, put an X in the box before the option that contains the most complete or accurate answer.

1. The family lived
    - ☐ a. in the middle of the city.
    - ☐ b. in a newly built suburb.
    - ☐ c. on a farm.
    - ☐ d. in a rich suburb near the lakeshore.

2. David Mamet's sister was
    - ☐ a. his twin.
    - ☐ b. a few years older than he.
    - ☐ c. a few years younger than he.
    - ☐ d. about ten years younger than he.

3. This story is told
    - ☐ a. through a series of events happening at different times.
    - ☐ b. in strict time order.
    - ☐ c. in spatial order.
    - ☐ d. through conversations among the family members.

4. A title that could summarize this story would be
    - ☐ a. Fighting with My Sister.
    - ☐ b. An Unhappy Family.
    - ☐ c. Growing Up on the Prairie.
    - ☐ d. Starting at a New School.

5. Mamet's feelings about the high school were
    - ☐ a. very positive.
    - ☐ b. that it gave him a bad education.
    - ☐ c. that it had some unrealistic ideas about honesty.
    - ☐ d. that it should have concentrated more on sports.

6. The rule of conduct that Mamet's mother believed in was
    - ☐ a. you must always obey or you will be punished.
    - ☐ b. children should never speak at the dinner table.
    - ☐ c. if you lie it was even worse than disobeying.
    - ☐ d. slapping is the only way to control an arrogant child.

7. Mamet finds the "family joke" to be
    - ☐ a. something that kept the family members close.
    - ☐ b. a sign of his stepfather's good sense of humor.
    - ☐ c. similar to jokes that every family plays on its members.
    - ☐ d. something that really wasn't very funny at all.

8. The tone of this article is
    - ☐ a. unconcerned.
    - ☐ b. forgiving.
    - ☐ c. amusing.
    - ☐ d. angry.

9. Mamet's stepfather
    - ☐ a. was a house builder.
    - ☐ b. had a bad temper.
    - ☐ c. liked his stepdaughter better than his stepson.
    - ☐ d. wanted children of his own.

10. The description in the last paragraph of this selection appeals mostly to the sense of
    - ☐ a. sight.
    - ☐ b. hearing.
    - ☐ c. smell.
    - ☐ d. taste.

Comprehension Skills Key

1. recalling specific facts	6. making a judgment
2. retaining concepts	7. making an inference
3. organizing facts	8. recognizing tone
4. understanding the main idea	9. understanding characters
5. drawing a conclusion	10. appreciating literary forms

VOCABULARY—PART TWO

Write the word that makes the most sense in each sentence.

adjacent proprietary
innovations utopian
prospect

1. The family was excited about the
   _____ of moving to a new home.

2. Because the house had just been built, there were
   many _____ in its construction.

3. The house was _____ to a corn-
   field on one side; on the other side was a row of
   houses.

4. The builders wanted to create a[n]
   _____ community where every-
   thing was clean, well-organized, and beautiful.

5. Owning such a wonderful house brought out the
   _____ feelings in many people.

engendered camaraderie
avert proximity
signal

6. Considering that the family expected living in the
   new house to change their attitudes, it was
   _____ how little changed.

7. They expected to like each other better, but a
   sense of _____ never developed
   among them.

8. They thought they would like open spaces, but
   their _____ to an empty cornfield
   made them lonesome.

9. They thought living in a big house would
   _____ arguments, but they
   argued anyway.

10. The house never _____ feelings
    in family members that they couldn't bring into
    existence by themselves.

Comprehension [_____]

Vocabulary [_____]

17

UNDERSTANDING THROUGH WRITING

Why do you think David Mamet particularly remembers the raking episode? Write a brief explanation of what you think. Use information from the story to support what you say.

_____

_____

_____

_____

_____

_____

_____

_____

_____

BUILDING STUDY SKILLS

Read the following passage and answer the questions that follow it.

How to Preview, I

Previewing is known by many names. It is called *surveying* and *prereading* too. The first three steps in previewing are as follows:

1. Read the Title. You would normally do that before reading a selection, but in previewing you should also be aware of what you can *learn* from the title. Not only can you learn the author's subject; you can frequently learn how he or she *feels* about that subject. W. H. Auden once wrote an essay entitled "Poetry Must Praise." From the title you can discern the author's feelings, and you would expect to read arguments supporting his position and illustrations demonstrating his case. The title "The Dread Tomato Addiction," on the other hand, suggests that the article will very likely contain humor or satire.

Headlines and titles are thought to be quite influential by authors and editors. In fact, many magazines survive on the surprise or shock value of the titles of their articles. The title can help you approach the selection intelligently by hinting at what to expect.

2. Read the Subheads. In textbooks especially, and in many magazines as well, subheads follow the title to give the reader more information on the subject. In textbooks, subheads often take the form of one-line summaries of the chapter—for example, "Here's what we are going to cover." In magazines, "teaser" statements follow the title to further spark the reader's interest. Look for subheads whenever you are previewing.

3. Read the Illustrations. If a picture or illustration accompanies the article, don't glance at it and move on. *Read* it—that is, interpret it to learn what you can about the content of the article. You have no doubt heard it said that a picture is worth a thousand words. You can prove the worth of that observation by studying the illustrations when previewing.

1. The first step in previewing is

   _____ .

2. The first step can not only identify the author's subject, but it may also convey his or her

   _____ about the subject.

3. If David Mamet had used a title like *Living and Loving in Our Family*, it would have suggested that he was going to praise rather than

   _____ his parents.

4. The subheads in textbooks frequently give a one-line _____ of the chapters.

5. _____ , such as the one of the leaves that accompanies this article, may give some clue about the content of the article.

18

3

Borderline

Kathleen Norris

READING PURPOSE—
In this selection the writer explains what makes her sister special. As you read, try to understand the relationship between the two women.

VOCABULARY—PART ONE

All of these words are in the selection you are about to read. Study each word and its meaning. Then answer the questions below. As you read the selection, notice how each vocabulary word is used.

induced: brought on

notoriety: fame

advocates: those who defend or support a person or idea

fabricate: make up; pretend to have

resorted: turned for help

tenacity: firmness; determination

adept: skilled; proficient

discern: notice; understand

incessantly: unceasingly; constantly

mortality: condition of being sure to die at some time

---

1. Which word might describe what you do when you pretend to have a bad cold?

   _____

2. Which word could describe a person who is very good at playing the piano or using a power tool?

   _____

3. Which word could describe how a person talks if no one else ever gets a chance to say anything?

   _____

4. Which word might describe the attention and recognition a movie star receives?

   _____

5. Which word might describe people who hand out leaflets on the street corner in order to get votes for their candidate?

   _____

1 Since my book *Dakota* became a surprise best-seller in 1993, I've received thousands of letters responding to it. Along with the reviews, these responses have been, for the most part, positive, and often so enthusiastic that I wonder if the person has read the same book that I wrote. I was enormously relieved, then, to receive the following from my sister Becky: "How are you? Everyone here talks about you and your book. I feel left out. I tried to read it, but it was boring."…

2 Becky's letter was a godsend. Reading it over, I laughed myself silly, and found myself released from much of the tension <u>induced</u> by sudden <u>notoriety</u>, the rigors of a book tour stretched out over three years: too much travel, too much literary hoo-ha.

3 Becky's life has been a kind of desert. When she was born, the doctors at Bethesda Naval Hospital gave my mother too strong a dose of sedative. Having already given birth to two children, she knew something was wrong when she couldn't push enough to release Becky from the birth canal. Precious oxygen was lost. My mother recalls one doctor saying to another, "You got yourself into this mess; let's see you get yourself out." While the doctors squabbled, my sister's brain was irreversibly damaged.

4 Becky is diagnosed as "borderline." She is intelligent enough to comprehend what happened to her when she was born. She is not intelligent enough to do mathematical computation. A tutor my parents hired when Becky was about ten years old told us that Becky could grasp a concept long enough to work out several problems in the course of an hour-long session, but that by the next week she'd have forgotten what she'd learned and have to start from scratch. Her elementary schools were just passing her along; there were no "special ed" programs then, and no one knew what to do with her, where she belonged. Becky's life has been lonely in ways that most of us could not comprehend.

5 Yet our family ties are strong, and for years we've acted as Becky's <u>advocates</u> within the educational and medical establishment, sometimes taking consolation in the fact that Becky is a good enough judge of human nature to wrap psychiatrists round her little finger. Several times, when she's been given a tranquilizer or some other drug she didn't like, she's learned enough about the contraindications[1] to <u>fabricate</u> symptoms so that the doctor would be forced to change her prescription. When she realized that alcoholic families were fashionable—at least "in" with therapists—she convinced one psychologist that her mother was an alcoholic. (My mother is the sort of person who, on a big night out, once or twice a year, drinks a tiny bit of créme de menthe.) In order to survive in her desert, my sister has often <u>resorted</u> to being a con artist: you get what you want by telling people what they want to hear.

6 She learned all of this, of course, in the bosom of our family. Our parents decided when Becky was very young that she didn't belong in an institution, but with us. I believe that being raised with myself and a brother, both older, and one younger sister, was good for Becky; I know it was good for me. Very early on, I had to learn to respect Becky's intelligence, although it was very different from mine. I also came to respect her <u>tenacity</u>. When she was two years old, and learning to walk was still beyond her capabilities, she became <u>adept</u> at scooting around the house, always with a security blanket in hand. I also had to learn to <u>discern</u> the difference between what Becky was truly incapable of knowing, and what she was simply trying to get by with. When she destroyed my first lipstick by writing with it on a brick wall, I took off after her. She yelled, "You can't hit me, I'm retarded." She learned that she was wrong.

7 When I was in high school I began to discover how much my sister and I had in common. We were both in difficult situations—I was a shy, ungainly newcomer at a prep school where many of the students had been together since kindergarten, and Becky had a particularly unsympathetic teacher. On coming home from school, she'd immediately go to her room and play mindless rock music—"Monster Mash" is one that I recall—while she danced around her room (and sometimes on her bed). She talked to herself, <u>incessantly</u> and loudly. The family accepted all this as something Becky needed to do.

8 One day, as Becky carried on her usual "conversations," with her teacher, with other girls in her class, with a boy who'd made fun of her, I was doing homework in the room next door and realized that I, too, needed release from daily tensions,

---

[1]*contraindications:* signs or evidence that a medical treatment is inadvisable

a way to daydream through the failed encounters and make them come out right. Usually, I lost myself in reading or practicing the flute, but sometimes I listened to music—the Beach Boys, Verdi, Bob Dylan, Frank Sinatra—and imagined great careers for myself, great travels, great loves. I didn't have the nerve to stomp around my room and yell, as my sister was doing, but our needs were the same.

"To most people, my sister and I didn't seem to have much in common, but I knew…that we were remarkably alike."

9   We were both struggling with our otherness, although I suspect I did not know this then. Now that I'm a writer, it's clear to me. Rejection comes to everyone, of course, but for those who are markedly different from their peers, it is a daily reminder of that difference. To most people, my sister and I didn't seem to have much in common; but I knew from that day on that we were remarkably alike.

10   If nothing else, this insight helped me to survive the intensely competitive atmosphere of my prep school. I knew that getting a C on a test was not the worst thing in the world. And when I got an A, when my writing got praised by my English teacher, as it often did, I could put it in perspective. I knew there were other kinds of intelligence that were just as valuable; needs that could not be satisfied in school.

11   Our parents are nearing eighty years of age and, while they often seem to have more energy as the years go by, the fact of their <u>mortality</u> looms large for their children. Becky, God bless her, is incapable of hiding her fears. We went for a walk one Christmas Eve not long ago, and she said, out of the blue: "I don't want Mom and Dad to die. I worry about what will happen to me."

12   "It scares me too," I replied. "But *everyone* is scared to think about their parents dying." I'm not sure I convinced Becky on this point—she tends to think that she's alone in her suffering, and all too often in her life, that has been the case. But I believe I did manage to reassure her that her brother and sisters would not abandon her.

13   As we walked through a light Honolulu rain— bright sunlight, prickles of moisture on bare skin— I remembered the two little girls who used to hide in their rooms every afternoon after school. How good it is to have those difficult years behind us. Becky will tell you that she's "slow." I guess I've always been fast by comparison. What does it matter, on the borderline? We're middle-aged women now, and our parents are old. As for the future, human maturity being what it is, the slow process of the heart's awakening, I sometimes wonder if Becky is better equipped for it than I.

Starting Time

Finishing Time

Reading Time

Reading Rate

COMPREHENSION

Read the following questions and statements. For each one, put an X in the box before the option that contains the most complete or accurate answer.

1. Becky found her sister's best-selling book to be
   - ☐ a. exciting.
   - ☐ b. too hard for her to read.
   - ☐ c. insulting to the family.
   - ☐ d. boring.

2. The family believed that it was important for Becky to live
   - ☐ a. in the family home.
   - ☐ b. in a special group home.
   - ☐ c. in a hospital for the mentally ill.
   - ☐ d. in an apartment with her sister.

3. The time frame of this selection can be described as
   - ☐ a. beginning and ending in 1993.
   - ☐ b. beginning in 1993 and ending in 1996.
   - ☐ c. beginning in 1993 but then going back into the past.
   - ☐ d. ending in 1993.

4. The author sees her sister as
   - ☐ a. someone she has always competed with.
   - ☐ b. really no different from her at all.
   - ☐ c. different from her, but having her own skills and insights.
   - ☐ d. a person who deserves special treatment because of her problems.

5. Becky's problems are the result of
   - ☐ a. prescription drugs that her mother took during pregnancy.
   - ☐ b. her low self-esteem.
   - ☐ c. brain damage that occurred at her birth.
   - ☐ d. an infection that she got when she was six weeks old.

6. As schoolgirls, Becky and the author were alike in that
   - ☐ a. they both liked the same music.
   - ☐ b. they both often felt isolated and alone.
   - ☐ c. they both went to the same school.
   - ☐ d. they both worried about their parents getting old.

7. When the author talks about Becky's "desert," she is referring to her
   - ☐ a. need for sweets.
   - ☐ b. enjoyment of unusual vacation spots.
   - ☐ c. life in Hawaii.
   - ☐ d. feeling alone and different.

8. The general tone of this article is
   - ☐ a. humorous and sometimes even silly.
   - ☐ b. sympathetic but fair.
   - ☐ c. angry and jealous.
   - ☐ d. hopeful but worried.

9. As she is portrayed in paragraphs 5 and 6, Becky can be described as
   - ☐ a. clever in trying to get situations to work for her.
   - ☐ b. afraid to try new things.
   - ☐ c. eager to go out and face the world by herself.
   - ☐ d. loud and boisterous.

10. This selection is
    - ☐ a. a short story.
    - ☐ b. part of a novel.
    - ☐ c. an autobiography told from Becky's point of view.
    - ☐ d. a memoir.

Comprehension Skills Key

1. recalling specific facts
2. retaining concepts
3. organizing facts
4. understanding the main idea
5. drawing a conclusion
6. making a judgment
7. making an inference
8. recognizing tone
9. understanding characters
10. appreciating literary forms

VOCABULARY—PART TWO

Write the word that makes the most sense in each sentence.

fabricate	**resorted**
adept	**discern**
incessantly	

1. When their child was born "different," Becky's parents could have _____ to quacks or faith healers.

2. What they needed was someone _____ at caring for special children.

3. Becky could not always _____ information from books.

4. When nervous, she could get very talkative and chatter on _____ .

5. If telling the truth wasn't convenient, she would sometimes _____ stories.

induced	**notoriety**
advocates	**mortality**
tenacity	

6. As her parents got very old, Becky worried about their _____ .

7. They had always been her _____, supporting her in whatever she did.

8. They encouraged her _____ in situations in which it would have been easy to give up.

9. They also helped her deal with her sister's _____ from her best-selling book.

10. Becky sometimes feared that one of them would suffer a heart attack _____ by worry over her future.

Comprehension [ ]

Vocabulary [ ]

UNDERSTANDING THROUGH WRITING

What do you think will happen to Becky after her parents die? Write down your ideas. Try to use information from the selection to back up what you say.

_____

_____

_____

_____

_____

_____

_____

_____

_____

_____

_____

BUILDING STUDY SKILLS

Read the following passage and answer the questions that follow it.

How to Preview, II

You have seen how previewing is necessary for intelligent reading. The first three steps are (1) read the title, (2) read the subheads, and (3) look at the illustrations. Here are the last three steps:

4. Read the Opening Paragraph. The first paragraph is the author's opening, his or her first opportunity to address the audience. This paragraph is also called the introductory paragraph because it is precisely that—an introduction to the article or chapter. Opening paragraphs are written with different purposes in mind. Some authors announce what they plan to say in the main body of the work. Others tell why they are writing the article or chapter and why it is important. Still others will do what speakers do—start with a story or anecdote to set the stage. This provides the setting or mood needed to present their material.

5. Read the Closing Paragraph. The next step in previewing is to read the last paragraph. That is where authors have a last chance to address the reader. If they have any closing remarks or final thoughts, or if they wish to reemphasize or restate principal thoughts or arguments, they will do so in the closing paragraph. Since it is the closing paragraph, it must express concluding or summarizing thoughts. You will see what authors consider important in their closing paragraphs.

6. Skim Through. Finally, to complete your preview, quickly skim the article or chapter to get a sense of what is in it. Watch for headings and numbers that indicate important elements of the author's presentation. You may, for example, learn that the material is broken down into four or five major aspects; that knowledge will be helpful when you are reading.

1. The first paragraph is usually an

   _____ to the article.

2. Authors use the first paragraph to announce their plans, to give their reason for writing the article, or to set the stage with a story or

   _____ .

3. The author of "Borderline," for example, sets the stage with a story about an amusing

   _____ she received from her sister.

4. In the concluding paragraph, the author may restate main points or make _____ remarks.

5. When you preview, you should quickly

   _____ the article to get a sense of what is in it.

Becoming Number One

Jill Nelson

READING PURPOSE—
In this selection the writer recalls how her father's beliefs influenced her as she was growing up. Read to find out what her father thought and how she reacted to it.

VOCABULARY—PART ONE

All of these words are in the selection you are about to read. Study each word and its meaning. Then answer the questions below. As you read the selection, notice how each vocabulary word is used.

intones: speaks in a singsong voice

revelation: disclosure of divine truth

rapt: enchanted; lost in delight

asserted: claimed

eroding: wearing away

coyly: acting more shyly than one really is

phallic: symbolizing or representing a penis

recurring: occurring over and over

communion: a close spiritual relationship

admonishing: warning; scolding

1. Which word might tell what a preacher does when he repeats certain phrases in a sort of chant?

   _____

2. Which word could describe what water constantly beating against rocks is doing to them?

   _____

3. Which word describes what a teacher is probably doing if she is shaking her finger at a group of little children?

   _____

4. Which word might describe a dream that you have every night for a week?

   _____

5. Which word might describe your reaction if you enjoy a movie so much that you are completely taken in by its plot?

   _____

1   That night I dream about my father, but it is really more a memory than a dream.

2   "Number one! Not two! Number one!" my father intones from the head of the breakfast table. The four of us sit at attention, two on each side of the ten-foot teak expanse, our brown faces rigid. At the foot, my mother looks up at my father, the expression on her face a mixture of pride, anxiety, and could it be, boredom? I am twelve. It is 1965.

3   "You kids have got to be, not number two," he roars, his dark face turning darker from the effort to communicate. He holds up his index and middle fingers. "But number(" here, he pauses dramatically, a preacher going for revelation, his four children a rapt congregation, my mother a smitten church sister. "Number one!"

4   These last words he shouts while lowering his index finger. My father has great, big black hands, long, perfectly shaped fingers with oval nails so vast they seem landscapes all their own. The half moons leading to the cuticle take up most of the nail and seem ever encroaching, threatening to swallow up first his fingertips, then his whole hand. I always wondered if he became a dentist just to mess with people by putting those enormous fingers in their mouths, each day surprising his patients and himself by the delicacy of the work he did.

5   Years later my father told me that when a woman came to him with an infant she asserted was his, he simply looked at the baby's hands. If they lacked the size, enormous nails, and half-moon cuticles like an ocean eroding the shore of the fingers, he dismissed them.

6   Early on, what I remember of my father were Sunday morning breakfasts and those hands, index finger coyly lowering, leaving the middle finger standing alone.

7   When he shouted "Number one!" that finger seemed to grow, thicken and harden, thrust up and at us, a phallic symbol to spur us, my sister Lynn, fifteen, brothers Stanley and Ralph, thirteen and nine, on to greatness, to number oneness. My father's rich, heavy voice rolled down the length of the table, breaking and washing over our four trembling bodies….

8   I never went to church with my family. While other black middle-class families journeyed to Baptist church on Sundays, both to thank the Lord for their prosperity and donate a few dollars to the less fortunate brethren they'd left behind, we had what was reverentially known as "Sunday breakfast." That was our church.

9   In the dining room of the eleven-room apartment we lived in, the only black family in a building my father had threatened to file a discrimination suit to get into, my father delivered the gospel according to him. The recurring theme was the necessity that each of us be "number one," but my father preached about what was on his mind: current events, great black heroes, lousy black sell-outs, our responsibility as privileged children, his personal family history.

10 His requirements were the same as those at church: that we be on time, not fidget, hear and heed the gospel, and give generously. But Daddy's church boasted no collection plate; dropping a few nickels into a bowl would have been too easy. Instead, my father asked that we absorb his lessons and become what he wanted us to be, number one. He never told us what that meant or how to get there. It was years before I was able to forgive my father for not being more specific. It was even longer before I understood and accepted that he couldn't be.

11 Like most preachers, my father was stronger on imagery, oratory, and instilling fear than he was on process. I came away from fifteen years of Sunday breakfasts knowing that to be number two was not enough, and having no idea what number one was or how to become it, only that it was better.

12 When I was a kid, I just listened, kept a sober face, and tried to understand what was going on. Thanks to my father, my older sister Lynn and I, usually at odds, found spiritual communion. The family dishwashers, our spirits met wordlessly as my father talked. We shared each other's anguish as we watched egg yolk harden on plates, sausage fat congeal, chicken livers separate silently from gravy.

13 We all had our favorite sermons. "You think we're doing well?" my father would begin, looking into each of our four faces. We knew better than to venture a response. For my father, even now, conversations are lectures. Please save your applause—and questions—until the end.

14 "And we are," he'd answer his own query. "We live on West End Avenue, I'm a professional, your mother doesn't *have* to work, you all go to private school, we go to Martha's Vineyard in the summer. But what we have, we have because 100,000 other black people haven't made it. Have nothing! Live like dogs!"

15 My father has a wonderfully expressive voice. When he said dogs, you could almost hear them whimpering. In my head, I saw an uncountable mass of black faces attached to the bodies of mutts, scrambling to elevate themselves to a better life. For some reason, they were always on 125th Street, under the Apollo Theatre marquee. Years later, when I got political and decided to be the number-one black nationalist, I was thrilled by the notion that my father might have been inspired by Claude McKay's poem that begins, "If we must die, let it not be like dogs."

16 "There is a quota system in this country for black folks, and your mother and me were allowed to make it," my father went on. It was hard to imagine anyone allowing my six-foot-three, suave, smart…father to do anything. Maybe his use of the word was a rhetorical device.

17 "Look around you," he continued. With the long arm that supported his heavy hand he indicated the dining room. I looked around. At the eight-foot china cabinet gleaming from the weekly oiling administered by Margie, our housekeeper, filled to bursting with my maternal grandmother's china and silver. At the lush green carpeting, the sideboard that on holidays sagged from the weight of cakes, pies, and cookies, at the paintings on the walls. We were living kind of good, I thought. That notion lasted only an instant.

18 My father's arm slashed left. It was as though he had stripped the room bare. I could almost hear the china crashing to the floor, all that teak splintering, silver clanging.

19 "…What we have, compared to what Rockefeller and the people who rule the world have, is nothing. Nothing! Not even good enough for his dog. You four have to remember that and do better than I have. Not just for yourselves, but for our people, black people. You have to be number one."

20 My father went on, but right about there was where my mind usually started drifting. I was

"I like to think he was simply saying, like the army, 'Be all that you can be,' but I'm still not sure."

entranced by the image of Rockefeller's dog—which I imagined to be a Corgi or Afghan or Scottish Terrier—bladder and rectum full to bursting, sniffing around the green carpet of our dining room, refusing to relieve himself.

21 The possible reasons for this fascinated me. Didn't he like green carpets? Was he used to defecating on rare Persian rugs and our 100 percent wool carpeting wasn't good enough? Was it because we were black? But weren't dogs colorblind?

22 I've spent a good part of my life trying to figure out what my father meant by number one. Born poor and dark in Washington, [D.C.], I think he was trying, in his own way, to protect us from the crushing assumptions of failure that he and his generation grew up with. I like to think he was simply saying, like the army, "Be all that you can be," but I'm still not sure. For years, I was haunted by the specter of number two gaining on me, of never having a house nice enough for Rockefeller dog shit, of my father's middle finger admonishing me. It's hard to move forward when you're looking over your shoulder.

23 When I was younger, I didn't ask my father what he meant. By the time I was confident enough to ask, my father had been through so many transformations—from dentist to hippie to lay guru—that he'd managed to forget, or convince himself he'd forgotten, those Sunday morning sermons. When I brought them up he'd look blank, his eyes would glaze over, and he'd say something like, "Jill, what are you talking about? With your dramatic imagination you should have been an actress."

24 But I'm not an actress, I'm a journalist, my father's daughter. I've spent a good portion of my life trying to be a good race woman and number one at the same time. Tomorrow, I go to work at the *Washington Post* magazine, a first. Falling asleep, I wonder if that's the same as being number one.

Starting Time [   ]

Finishing Time [   ]

Reading Time [   ]

Reading Rate [   ]

COMPREHENSION

Read the following questions and statements. For each one, put an X in the box before the option that contains the most complete or accurate answer.

1. How many children were in the author's family?
   - ☐ a. two
   - ☐ b. three
   - ☐ c. four
   - ☐ d. five

2. The father used Sunday breakfast as
   - ☐ a. an opportunity to lecture his children.
   - ☐ b. a time for family prayer.
   - ☐ c. a time to settle the children's arguments.
   - ☐ d. an opportunity to criticize his wife.

3. In developing her story, the author
   - ☐ a. begins at the beginning of an event and works toward the end.
   - ☐ b. presents Sunday-breakfast memories in no particular order.
   - ☐ c. uses order of importance, giving the most important details last.
   - ☐ d. uses spatial order.

4. A good summary of the author's feelings about breakfast with her father is that
   - ☐ a. she knew he was urging his children on, but she wasn't quite sure what his message was.
   - ☐ b. she knew that to him being number one meant ruthlessly stepping on other people.
   - ☐ c. she realized her father had a lot of resentment toward Nelson Rockefeller.
   - ☐ d. she realized that her father had a lot of resentment toward all whites.

5. What does the father mean in paragraph 17 when he says there is a "quota system…for black folks"?
   - ☐ a. Only a certain number of blacks are allowed to succeed in white society.
   - ☐ b. All companies have to hire a certain number of blacks.
   - ☐ c. Most apartment buildings in their area were lived in by whites only.
   - ☐ d. Blacks have to struggle with other minority groups to get jobs.

6. The father mentioned Rockefeller's dog to show that
   - ☐ a. some people have pets with very poor manners.
   - ☐ b. his own children weren't as well off as they thought they were.
   - ☐ c. people would take advantage of you if you weren't constantly on your guard.
   - ☐ d. certain kinds of dogs didn't like black people.

7. When the author says "It was years before I could forgive my father for not being more specific," she suggests that her father's sermons made her feel
   - ☐ a. mistrustful.
   - ☐ b. sinful.
   - ☐ c. unimportant.
   - ☐ d. angry.

8. The author uses a tone in this selection that
   - ☐ a. shows how angry her father made her.
   - ☐ b. makes clear how boring the Sunday sermons were.
   - ☐ c. shows her disgust with white people.
   - ☐ d. presents her father in a humorous way.

9. As a result of her father's lectures, the author grew up to be
   - ☐ a. angry.
   - ☐ b. self-confident.
   - ☐ c. insecure.
   - ☐ d. jealous.

10. Throughout the selection, the writer's father is compared to a
    - ☐ a. college instructor.
    - ☐ b. dentist.
    - ☐ c. hippie.
    - ☐ d. preacher.

Comprehension Skills Key

1. recalling specific facts
2. retaining concepts
3. organizing facts
4. understanding the main idea
5. drawing a conclusion
6. making a judgment
7. making an inference
8. recognizing tone
9. understanding characters
10. appreciating literary forms

VOCABULARY—PART TWO

Write the word that makes the most sense in each sentence.

revelation   **coyly**
phallic   **recurring**
admonishing

1. The father spoke in a loud, serious voice, as if he were preaching _____ from the heavens.

2. He spent a lot of time giving warnings to his children, _____ them to try harder.

3. A _____ theme in just about every lecture he gave was that they must become number one.

4. The father must have known that holding up his middle finger was a _____ symbol.

5. Still, he held it up _____ , pretending not to notice what he was signaling.

rapt   **asserted**
eroding   **intones**
communion

6. In the author's dreams, her father _____ his message as if he has recorded it.

7. His constant repetition of that message soon began _____ her resistance to it.

8. Ganging together to defend themselves brought the author and her sister into a kind of _____ .

9. Usually they listened to him with boredom rather than with _____ attention.

10. Later, the author _____ that her father had really confused her, a claim her sister would agree with.

Comprehension [   ]

Vocabulary [   ]

UNDERSTANDING THROUGH WRITING

What do you think the author's father meant by "number one"? Write a brief explanation of your ideas. Support what you say with information from the story.

_____

_____

_____

_____

_____

_____

_____

BUILDING STUDY SKILLS

Read the following passage and answer the questions that follow it.

Question the Author

You've probably heard it said that you'll never learn if you don't ask questions.

Why is a willingness to ask questions associated with learning? The answer is that learning is not a passive process; it is something we *do*. Learning is a possession. We must go after it and seek it out. That is why we say that questioning is part of learning.

Following your previewing, ask questions like "What can I expect to learn from this chapter or article? Based on my previewing, what are some of the topics likely to be presented? What will the author tell me about this subject?" Such questions frame the subject and provide a general outline to be filled in when reading.

Another thing to discover from questioning is the author's method of presentation. There are many methods an author can use. Some may ask questions and answer them, using that method to make the subject easier to learn. Some may give details or describe and illustrate. Others may compare and contrast, while still others use sequential or historical order. Many use a combination of techniques. Whatever the method, discover it and put it to use when studying.

In many books the questions are there waiting to be used. Check your textbooks. Are there questions following the chapters? If so, use them during previewing to instill the questioning spirit so necessary to learning. Those questions tell what important points the author really expects you to learn in each chapter.

Develop the technique of questioning. Try whenever you study to create questions you expect to find answered.

1. In order to learn, it is necessary to

    _____ .

2. Ask yourself what you expect to

    _____ from the article.

3. One of your aims should be to discover the

    author's method of _____ .

4. In this selection, Jill Nelson gives details that paint

    a clear picture of her _____ .

5. Reading the questions that follow a chapter can

    help you understand what points the author thinks

    are _____ .

How We Kept Mother's Day

Stephen Leacock

> **R E A D I N G   P U R P O S E —**
> In this selection the writer tells how a family planned to be especially kind to the mother.
> Read to see how the plans actually worked out.

VOCABULARY—PART ONE

All of these words are in the selection you are about to read. Study each word and its meaning. Then answer the questions below. As you read the selection, notice how each vocabulary word is used.

notion: idea

becoming: attractive

aimlessness: lack of purpose or direction

reckoned: planned; figured

plug: work steadily

principally: mainly, particularly

verandah: a large porch

specimens: samples; examples

spare: save from labor or pain

humor: give in to the desires of a person

---

1. Which word names a place where people often like to sit on warm summer nights?

_____

2. Which word means the opposite of "not attractive"?

_____

3. Which word describes what you are doing if you go along with a friend's plans in order to keep her happy?

_____

4. Which word might describe the situation of a person who moves from one task to another without any firm plan for accomplishing anything?

_____

5. Which word might describe what you do if you work at the copying machine for forty-five minutes without a break?

_____

1   Of all the different ideas that have been started lately, I think that the very best is the <u>notion</u> of celebrating once a year "Mother's Day." I don't wonder that this is becoming such a popular day all over America and I am sure the idea will spread to England too.

2   It is especially in a big family like ours that such an idea takes hold. So we decided to have a special celebration of Mother's Day. We thought it a fine idea. It made us all realize how much Mother had done for us for years, and all the efforts and sacrifices that she had made for our sake.

3   So we decided that we'd make it a great day, a holiday for all the family, and do everything we could to make Mother happy. Father decided to take a holiday from his office so as to help in celebrating the day, and my sister Anne and I stayed home from college classes, and Mary and my brother Will stayed home from high school.

4   It was our plan to make it a day just like Xmas or any big holiday, and so we decided to decorate the house with flowers and with mottoes over the mantelpieces, and all that kind of thing. We got Mother to make mottoes and arrange the decorations, because she always does it at Xmas.

5   The two girls thought it would be a nice thing to dress in our very best for such a big occasion, and so they both got new hats. Mother trimmed both the hats, and they looked fine, and Father had bought four-in-hand silk ties for himself and us boys as a souvenir of the day to remember Mother by. We were going to get Mother a new hat too, but it turned out that she seemed to really like her old gray bonnet better than a new one, and both girls said that it was awfully <u>becoming</u> to her.

6   Well, after breakfast we had it arranged as a surprise for Mother that we would hire a motor car and take her for a beautiful drive into the country. Mother is hardly ever able to have a treat like that, because we can only afford to keep one maid, and so Mother is busy in the house nearly all the time. And of course the country is so lovely now that it would be just grand for her to have a lovely morning, driving for miles and miles.

7   But on the very morning of the day we changed the plan a little bit, because it occurred to Father that a thing it would be better to do even than to take Mother for a motor drive would be to take her fishing. Father said that as the car was hired and paid for, we might just as well use it for a drive up into hills where the streams are. As Father said, if you just go out driving without any object, you have a sense of <u>aimlessness</u>, but if you are going to fish, there is a definite purpose in front of you to heighten the enjoyment.

8   So we all felt that it would be nicer for Mother to have a definite purpose; and anyway, it turned out that Father had just got a new rod the day before, which made the idea of fishing all the more appropriate, and he said that Mother could use it if she wanted to; in fact, he said it was practically for her, only Mother said she would much rather watch him fish and not try to fish herself.

9   So we got everything arranged for the trip, and we got Mother to cut up some sandwiches and make up a sort of lunch in case we got hungry, though of course we were to come back home to a big dinner in the middle of the day, just like Xmas or New Year's Day. Mother packed it all up in a basket for us ready to go in the motor.

10   Well, when the car came to the door, it turned out that there hardly seemed as much room in it as we had supposed, because we hadn't <u>reckoned</u> on Father's fishing basket and the rods and the lunch, and it was plain enough that we couldn't all get in.

11   Father said not to mind him, he said that he could just as well stay at home, and that he was sure that he could put in the time working in the garden; he said that there was a lot of rough dirty work that he could do, like digging a trench for the garbage, that would save hiring a man, and so he said that he'd stay home; he said that we were not to let the fact of his not having a real holiday for three years stand in our way; he wanted us to go right ahead and be happy and have a big day, and not to mind him. He said that he could <u>plug</u> away all day, and in fact he said he'd been a fool to think there'd be any holiday for him.

12   But of course we all felt that it would never do to let Father stay home, especially as we knew he would make trouble if he did. The two girls, Anne and Mary, would gladly have stayed and helped the maid get dinner, only it seemed such a pity to, on a lovely day like this, having their new hats. But they both said that Mother had only to say the word, and they'd gladly stay home and work. Will and I would have dropped out, but unfortunately we wouldn't have been any use in getting the dinner.

13   So in the end it was decided that Mother would stay home and just have a lovely restful day round the house, and get the dinner. It turned out anyway

that Mother doesn't care for fishing, and also it was just a little bit cold and fresh out of doors, though it was lovely and sunny, and Father was rather afraid that Mother might take cold if she came.

14   He said he would never forgive himself if he dragged Mother round the country and let her take a severe cold at

"He said it was our duty to try and let Mother get all the rest she could."

a time when she might be having a beautiful rest. He said it was our duty to try and let Mother get all the rest and quiet that she could, after all that she had done for all of us, and he said that that was <u>principally</u> why he had fallen in with this idea of a fishing trip, so as to give Mother a little quiet. He said that young people seldom realize how much quiet means to people who are getting old. As to himself, he could still stand the racket, but he was glad to shelter Mother from it.

15   So we all drove away with three cheers for Mother, and Mother stood and watched us from the <u>verandah</u> for as long as she could see us, and Father waved his hand back to her every few minutes till he hit his hand on the back edge of the car, and then said that he didn't think that Mother could see us any longer.

16   Well, we had the loveliest day up among the hills that you could possibly imagine, and Father caught such big <u>specimens</u> that he felt sure that Mother couldn't have landed them anyway, if she had been fishing for them, and Will and I fished too, and the two girls met quite a lot of people that they knew as we drove along, and there were some young men friends of theirs that they met along the stream and talked to, and so we all had a splendid time.

17   It was quite late when we got back, nearly seven o'clock in the evening, but Mother had guessed that we would be late, so she had kept back the dinner so as to have it just nicely ready and hot for us. Only first she had to get towels and soap for Father and clean things for him to put on, because he always gets so messed up with fishing, and that

kept Mother busy for a little while, that and helping the girls get ready.

18   But at last everything was ready, and we sat down to the grandest kind of dinner—roast turkey and all sorts of things like on Xmas Day. Mother had to get up and down a good bit during the meal fetching things back and forward, but at the end Father noticed it and said she simply mustn't do it, that he wanted her to <u>spare</u> herself and he got up and fetched the walnuts over from the sideboard himself.

19   The dinner lasted a long while, and was great fun, and when it was over all of us wanted to help clear the things up and wash the dishes, only Mother said that she would really much rather do it, and so we let her, because we wanted just for once to <u>humor</u> her.

20   It was quite late when it was all over, and when we all kissed Mother before going to bed, she said it had been the most wonderful day in her life, and I think there were tears in her eyes. So we all felt awfully repaid for all that we had done.

Starting Time	
Finishing Time	
Reading Time	
Reading Rate	

COMPREHENSION

Read the following questions and statements. For each one, put an X in the box before the option that contains the most complete or accurate answer.

1. At the end of dinner Father
   - ☐ a. got the walnuts.
   - ☐ b. showed Mother the fish he had caught.
   - ☐ c. thanked Mother for cooking the meal.
   - ☐ d. told the children to go to bed.

2. Mother's Day was created to be a
   - ☐ a. business holiday.
   - ☐ b. replacement for Christmas.
   - ☐ c. day of recognition.
   - ☐ d. holiday from school.

3. The events in this story occur
   - ☐ a. over a period of several days.
   - ☐ b. from one evening till the next evening.
   - ☐ c. from one morning till the end of the day.
   - ☐ d. from one afternoon till the end of the day.

4. Another title that might fit this story is
   - ☐ a. A Day of Celebration.
   - ☐ b. What Does Mother Get Out of Mother's Day?
   - ☐ c. Mother Stays Home.
   - ☐ d. The Establishment of a New Holiday.

5. The reader first suspects that Mother's Day would be a busy workday for Mother when the
   - ☐ a. children asked her to do the decorations.
   - ☐ b. girls bought new hats.
   - ☐ c. boys bought silk ties to remember her by.
   - ☐ d. decision was made to organize a fishing outing.

6. Internal evidence suggests that the events of the selection took place in the
   - ☐ a. early 1800s.
   - ☐ b. middle 1800s.
   - ☐ c. early 1900s.
   - ☐ d. middle 1900s.

7. Father's offer to stay home was
   - ☐ a. an obvious strategy to get his way.
   - ☐ b. an expression of genuine concern.
   - ☐ c. reasonable, considering the work he had to do.
   - ☐ d. his contribution to Mother's Day.

8. The selection is meant to be
   - ☐ a. offensive.
   - ☐ b. educational.
   - ☐ c. controversial.
   - ☐ d. humorous.

9. Mother is portrayed as
   - ☐ a. demanding.
   - ☐ b. foolish.
   - ☐ c. accommodating.
   - ☐ d. athletic.

10. This selection is
    - ☐ a. a biography.
    - ☐ b. a piece of fiction.
    - ☐ c. an autobiography.
    - ☐ d. a true story told to prove a point.

Comprehension Skills Key

1. recalling specific facts	6. making a judgment
2. retaining concepts	7. making an inference
3. organizing facts	8. recognizing tone
4. understanding the main idea	9. understanding characters
5. drawing a conclusion	10. appreciating literary forms

VOCABULARY—PART TWO

Write the word that makes the most sense in each sentence.

plug   **verandah**
notion   **spare**
reckoned

1. Father wasn't sure whether he was right, but he
   _____ that Mother needed a day
   off.

2. The more he thought about it, the more he
   believed his _____ was a good
   one.

3. He often watched her _____
   away at some household job for hours.

4. She was always indoors working, hardly ever
   even having a chance to go out and sit on the
   _____ .

5. To _____ her a day's work, he
   decided to leave the house and not clutter up
   things for her.

humor   **principally**
specimens   **aimlessness**
becoming

6. Out on the road, Father didn't want
   _____ to control him, so he
   quickly settled on a specific destination.

7. The children weren't sure they wanted to go fishing, but they went along with his plan to
   _____ him.

8. Within an hour, he had several huge
   _____ caught and preserved in
   ice.

9. Plump and rosy colored, these fish would look

_____ to any good angler.

10. He had said the day off was for Mother, but it
    turned out to be _____ a holiday
    for himself.

    [ ]

Comprehension [ ]

Vocabulary

UNDERSTANDING THROUGH WRITING

There are several clues in this selection that let you know it was written a long time ago. Write a paragraph or two telling what some of those clues are.

_____

_____

_____

_____

_____

_____

_____

_____

_____

_____

_____

_____

BUILDING STUDY SKILLS

Read the following passage and answer the questions that follow it.

How to Concentrate, I

If you have trouble concentrating, consider yourself normal. Everyone at some time finds it hard to concentrate.

Concentrating means giving all your attention to the issue at hand. The trouble comes from distractions, things that keep us from paying attention to what we are doing.

Here are two ways to improve your ability to concentrate:

1. Increase Motivation. You have no doubt observed that you concentrate more easily when you are highly motivated. Motivation is one key to concentration. You are not easily distracted when you are really interested in something.

Things that involve some immediate and specific goal motivate people the most. It is not hard to study a driver's manual when the goal of getting a driver's license is at hand. The goal of passing tomorrow's test often helps students concentrate quite effectively the night before.

A good way to increase motivation, then, is to set a goal that means enough to help you develop the kind of concentration you need. Even a short-range goal might be enough to give you the motivation you need at the moment.

2. Prepare to Study. As simple as that may sound, it works. Prepare yourself properly and completely for the task of studying. Distractions will be a bother if you don't arrange to remove them, or to remove yourself from them. No one can concentrate in a noisy, busy room. Try to find a quiet, well-lighted spot equipped with a table and chair. Seated at the table, upright in the chair, you will be in the best posture for studying and concentrating.

1. Concentrating means giving something your exclusive _____ , shutting out everything else.

2. _____ is one key to concentration. We usually don't become distracted when we are interested.

3. It's easy to concentrate on something when you have a definite _____ in mind.

4. For example, if you knew in advance that you had to write about clues showing that the selection in this chapter is old, as you read you might have concentrated on items and events that set the story in the _____ .

5. You would probably go to read the selection in a place where you could remove yourself from _____ .

TOPIC REVIEW
React to Topic 1

Respond to one or more of these questions as your instructor directs.

1. The fathers in "Becoming Number One" and "How We Kept Mother's Day" had many differences, but in some ways they were quite similar. Make a list of at least two ways they were similar and two ways they were different.

_____

_____

_____

_____

_____

2. Using the information you developed in question 1, write a short paper comparing and contrasting the two fathers.

_____

_____

_____

_____

_____

3. In Building Study Skills 4 you learned about a study technique called "Question the Author." This technique can help you understand the author's intention in writing an article or chapter. Write three or four questions you would want to ask the author of "Spyglass" or of "Borderline." After each question, write how you think knowing the answer would help you understand the story better.

_____

_____

_____

_____

_____

4. Choose any two characters you have met in this unit. Imagine that they have been invited to speak at a conference called "The Joys of Family Life." Figure out a specific program for this conference. You will have to decide what each character's topic will be and whether they will speak separately or in a joint presentation. If you wish, you can design the flyer or program notes advertising this conference and put the speaker information into it.

_____

_____

_____

_____

_____

_____

_____

5. Today there are fewer families around with both a mother and a father living in the same house. What effect do you think broken families have on the children? Would children always be better off if they had two parents around? Write your opinion on these questions. Use specific examples to back up what you say.

_____

_____

_____

_____

_____

_____

6. Pretend that you had the chance to build a TV sitcom around the family characters in "Becoming Number One" or "Spyglass." Whom would you cast in each role in the story? Write down the actors you have chosen to play each part, and then write an explanation of why you selected those actors.

_____

_____

_____

_____

_____

_____

Our country is the world—our countrymen are all mankind.

—William Lloyd Garrison (1805–1879)

PLACES TO GO, PEOPLE TO SEE

6

Cajun Country

Charles Kuralt

READING PURPOSE—
This selection tells how life has changed for the Cajuns, settlers of French origin who live near New Orleans. Read to learn about their history and their life now.

VOCABULARY—PART ONE

All of these words are in the selection you are about to read. Study each word and its meaning. Then answer the questions below. As you read the selection, notice how each vocabulary word is used.

pluck: bravery; daring

rapture: extreme joy or pleasure

cadence: rhythm

lingo: special language; dialect

agrarian: countrylike; rustic

bayous: marshy inlets of a river or bay

meandered: wandered aimlessly

inferred: figured out from indirect clues

infectious: tending to spread from one person to another

sobering: causing to become serious or quiet

---

1. Which word names bodies of water?

2. Which word could describe the actions of a person who walks along the outside ledge of a high building?

3. Which word describes an area consisting of farms and occasional small towns?

4. Which word might describe the effect that bad news about a friend might have on you?

5. Which word might describe what you did if you took a walk that led nowhere in particular?

1   The Americans supplied the <u>pluck</u> of New Orleans, the Creoles supplied the <u>rapture</u>, the Africans provided the <u>cadence</u>. But that still doesn't account for a certain spice in the life of the city. The spice was the gift of the Cajuns.

2   The Cajuns came here in the first place because they didn't have any place else to go. More than two hundred years ago, the British expelled them from Nova Scotia, which the French called Acadia. Families were torn apart by the banishment. Thousands died at sea. Three or four thousand found their way to New Orleans, but not being city people, they moved on to the embracing safety of the swamp grass between the Mississippi and the Gulf. Here the Acadians became, in the <u>lingo</u> of their neighbors, Cajuns, and here many of them still live a sort of preindustrial <u>agrarian</u> life, farming and fishing and hunting in the <u>bayous</u> and letting the good times roll.

3   I have spent many contented hours in Cajun country, which is south and west of New Orleans in the once-unpopulated countryside. One day years ago, I pulled a chair up to an outdoor table at Harvey's Cypress Inn on the Bayou Chevreuil shortly after noon. When the sun went down, I was still there, still working at a meal of boiled crawfish, lightly seasoned, still tossing the shells overboard into the black water, still drinking beer and listening to Cajun fiddle tunes. It had to be a long meal because there is no way to eat crawfish in a hurry, and even if there were, it would be wrong to rush though such a pleasure. I don't have very many regrets about my life, but one of them is that I haven't spent more afternoons like that one.

4   I wouldn't want you to think the Cajuns are only eaters and drinkers and singers of songs. They have close, strong families. They support one another in time of trouble. They are devout Roman Catholics, up to a point. Cajuns believe in God, but they also believe God winks at a lot of little things.

5   I fell to wondering how Cajun habits and music and language are prospering these days, so I drove down through the swamps to Houma to see an acquaintance, Lenn Naquin. He and his brother, L. J., took me to lunch at Savoie's Restaurant, where Jimmy and Sandra Savoie, mistaking me for a celebrity, couldn't be stopped from preparing seafood gumbo, stuffed bell peppers, jambalaya,[1]

sautéed oysters, shrimp and fried perch, and serving all these dishes at once while Lenn and L. J. talked about Cajun life and how it has changed.

6   "It's the hunting and fishing life that appeals to me," L. J. said, "and I'd say that hasn't changed at all. I go deer hunting and duck hunting—mallards, wigeons, pintails, ringnecks. And I go fishing for red drum and speckled trout and bass and *sac-à-lait*—that's our Cajun spotted perch. The hunting and fishing right here in Terrebone Parish is the best I've heard of in the world. I went to Colorado one time with my son and asked at a sporting goods store where we could go trout fishing, and the guy took out a map and showed me a spot. He said, 'One man had a real good day here yesterday. He had three strikes and caught one fish.' I thought, good God, one fish is a good day? See, I'm used to catching a hundred fish before lunch."

7   "There's always something happening," Lenn said. "Gator season is September. Everybody tries to get an alligator tag and get 'em a gator. Well you can see why. I think this year, a gator was worth forty dollars a foot at the tanning company. You get you a twelve-foot gator and that's pretty good money."

8   "Shrimping is closed right now, so all the shrimpers are out trapping—nutria, otter, muskrat, some mink. That's until February, and then pretty soon the shrimping starts up again."

9   Jim Savoie, who had pulled up a chair, said, "Don't forget the crawfish."

10 Lenn said, "Oh, yes, the crawfish are just coming in, and they'll be good until about the first of June. During Lent, I still don't eat meat on Friday. Most people don't. It's not a sin anymore, people just don't do it, and the peak of crawfish season is during Lent. On Good Friday, every crawfish in the parish better fear for his life!"

11 "Ain't that the truth?" Jim Savoie said.

12 As our talk <u>meandered</u> on, though, I <u>inferred</u> that aside from the sporting aspects, Cajun life is being watered down by the influences from the world outside.

13 "We were brought up on the bayou," Lenn said. "It's Bayou Dularge, and we were probably the last generation to remember going out in our pirogues[2] and playing in the bayou all day, and then sitting out on the porch and talking all night. Traffic? You

---

[1]*jambalaya:* a spiced food dish consisting of ham, chicken, or shrimp; rice; and vegetables, especially tomatoes

[2]*pirogues:* dugout canoes

could hear a car coming for five miles in the silence of that place.

14 "We always went barefoot to school. We weren't poor—Daddy had the grocery store and the shrimpers would take whatever they needed and come back and pay their bill after they went shrimping. It was just that nobody wanted to wear shoes to school.

"'One old woman I know…calls the alligators up to be fed. There are still some old folks like that, but not as many as there used to be.'"

died off. Maybe there were never as many Cajun musicians as we thought."

22 Was the day coming, then, when Cajun country would be like every other place?

23 "Well, the day may be coming when Cajun country isn't here at all," Lenn said. "Terrebonne is the largest parish in Louisiana, but it gets smaller with every storm. The erosion is terrific. The Gulf is taking the land and we'll never get it back again."

15 "Our father spoke French—well, his customers, that's *all* they spoke. Out the end of the bayou where the road stops, the old families still speak French. But my generation was the first to have to speak English in school, that was the new rule. It was in the Fifties, I guess, all the school books came out in English.

16 "Now there's a big effort to teach the children French again to keep the heritage from dying. But they'd rather watch TV. It's too late, see."

17 "Ain't that the truth?" Jim Savoie said.

18 "I wish you could meet one old woman I know," Jim said. "She lives back in the swamp. She knows every bird and animal. She calls the alligators up to be fed. There are still some old folks like that, but not as many as there used to be."

19 "Ain't that the truth?" It was Lenn's turn to say it.

20 I asked about Cajun music, which is <u>infectious</u> and full of joy, and seems to be thriving at places like Prejean's in Lafayette and Fred's Lounge in Mamou. Fred's is the place you didn't think existed any more, the place your mama told you to stay away from when you were a kid, and you grew up and didn't and were never sorry.

21 "I love that music," Lenn agreed. "Daddy had a saloon beside the store. Friday was Crab Boil Night, and Sunday was Music Night, accordion and fiddle, I can hear it yet. But right around here, there's not much French music anymore, not even on the radio. Maybe the oil-field workers who came from outside never got into it, and our people

24 He sat for a minute shaking his head over that <u>sobering</u> fact. "The Lord giveth," he said, "and the Lord taketh away."

25 Then he brightened and smiled. "But here we still are," he said. "Everybody's friendly, you go around and see. Everybody will talk to you like they know you. That's the Cajun way, and most people here are still Cajuns. You can tell by their names. Just go down the road and read the names. All you'll see are Boudreaus, Heberts, Dupres, LeBlancs…

26 "And here we are eating at Savoie's. How do you like your food?"…

Starting Time

Finishing Time

Reading Time

Reading Rate

42

COMPREHENSION

Read the following questions and statements. For each one, put an X in the box before the option that contains the most complete or accurate answer.

1. The Cajuns originally came to Louisiana from
   ☐ a. France.
   ☐ b. Nova Scotia.
   ☐ c. Africa.
   ☐ d. New York.

2. The people that author Charles Kuralt talks to
   ☐ a. feel that Cajun life is changing in some ways.
   ☐ b. are raising their children to speak French.
   ☐ c. no longer enjoy hunting and fishing.
   ☐ d. feel uncomfortable talking to a "celebrity."

3. Kuralt presents information in this selection
   ☐ a. through a combination of explanation and conversation.
   ☐ b. through conversation only.
   ☐ c. through explanatory paragraphs only.
   ☐ d. by giving a detailed history of one family.

4. Which of the following is the best summary of this selection?
   ☐ a. Cajuns would rather sit around talking than work.
   ☐ b. Cajuns have a lot of unusual names for common objects.
   ☐ c. Cajuns have influenced the way food is cooked in New Orleans.
   ☐ d. Cajuns have a distinctive, but somewhat endangered, way of life.

5. The Cajuns in this selection
   ☐ a. enjoy visiting with city people.
   ☐ b. live in close contact with the land.
   ☐ c. know that they can make good money working in the nearby oil fields.
   ☐ d. are poor and struggling to survive.

6. One sign that life in the bayous is changing is that
   ☐ a. fishing and trapping aren't as good as they used to be.
   ☐ b. fewer children speak or understand French.
   ☐ c. Cajun music is becoming better known in other parts of the country.
   ☐ d. few people are cooking the traditional food.

7. A piece of advice the characters in this story seem to be giving is
   ☐ a. keep your children close to home.
   ☐ b. try to hold on to the old ways.
   ☐ c. don't expect everyone to be friendly.
   ☐ d. enjoy simple pleasures.

8. The tone of paragraph 3 in this selection is
   ☐ a. serious.
   ☐ b. sad.
   ☐ c. happy.
   ☐ d. humorous.

9. The author's feeling about life is that
   ☐ a. it is a mistake to stay more than a day in one place.
   ☐ b. one should stop to get a feel for places rather than race through.
   ☐ c. it's hard to get to know people of different cultures.
   ☐ d. when old customs die out, they should be allowed to go naturally.

10. The description at the end of paragraph 5 appeals mostly to the sense of
    ☐ a. sight.
    ☐ b. hearing.
    ☐ c. taste.
    ☐ d. touch.

Comprehension Skills Key

1. recalling specific facts
2. retaining concepts
3. organizing facts
4. understanding the main idea
5. drawing a conclusion
6. making a judgment
7. making an inference
8. recognizing tone
9. understanding characters
10. appreciating literary forms

VOCABULARY—PART TWO

Write the word that makes the most sense in each sentence.

pluck   **cadence**
bayous   **lingo**
agrarian

1. Cajuns, both men and women, enjoyed fishing in the _____ .

2. They preferred a(n) _____ lifestyle rather than one focused on the city.

3. The _____ they spoke was also distinct from city language.

4. It had a natural _____ that made it sound almost like music.

5. Cajuns feared little in the outdoor world; in fact, they often survived on their _____ .

meandered   **inferred**
rapture   **infectious**
sobering

6. Because of his companions' sad looks, the author _____ that they were unhappy about something.

7. He could tell that some _____ event was bringing sorrow into their lives.

8. Fearing that their unhappiness would become _____ , he asked them to talk about it before it spread.

9. At first the men could not get to the point; their conversation _____ from one idea to the next.

10. Finally, they said their sorrow would turn to _____ if he would only stay and have dinner with them.

Comprehension [ ]

Vocabulary [ ]

UNDERSTANDING THROUGH WRITING

Pretend that you had a chance to interview one or more of the Cajun men in this story. Write down several questions you would ask them. Then write what you think their answers might be.

_____
_____
_____
_____
_____
_____
_____
_____
_____
_____
_____
_____

BUILDING STUDY SKILLS

Read the following passage and answer the questions that follow it.

How to Concentrate, II

You have learned two techniques that you can use to improve concentration. They involve (1) increasing motivation, and (2) preparing to study. Here are three other techniques:

3. Set a Time. Have you ever noticed how timing brings out peak efficiency? Almost every athletic event is closely timed, or else the participants are competing against time. For instance, in track events the winner's time generates as much interest as does the place in which he or she finishes. Timing is a natural incentive to competitive athletes—they can't resist the challenge. You can make use of your sense of competition when you have an assignment to complete or a lesson to study. Set a time for the completion of the task. Your inclination to beat the clock may inspire the sustained concentration you need. Timing, put simply, builds concentration.

4. Pace the Assignment. Trying to do too much too soon will destroy concentration, not increase it. When an assignment is long, involved, and complex, it's best not to try to complete it at one sitting. Segment the task into twenty-minute parcels and spread out the periods of study. Returning to an unfinished task makes it easier to regain concentration, because you want to see the job completed. That desire to get the job done helps build the kind of concentration you need.

5. Organize the Task. One major reason students can't concentrate is that often the assignment is unplanned and vague. When that is the case, the assignment itself is a distraction. Through skills of Previewing and Questioning you should be able to organize the assignment into a series of related and specific tasks. List exactly what you wish to learn or accomplish in the designated periods of study. Then set up a time framework and stick to it.

1. To help concentration, it is suggested that you set a _____ for completion of the assignment.

2. If an assignment is very long or complex, divide it into sections, and _____ out the periods of study.

3. For instance, if you found this selection about the Cajuns difficult to read, you could have segmented it into two shorter _____ of time.

4. It is important to organize the assignment into a series of related and specific _____ before you begin.

5. One part of your plan for reading this selection should have been to consider your reading purpose, to learn something about the Cajun way of _____ .

7

Into the Kenyan Game Reserve

Michael Palin

READING PURPOSE—
In this selection, actor and author Michael Palin describes what he experiences during a safari in the African country of Kenya. Read to learn how things go for him.

VOCABULARY—PART ONE

All of these words are in the selection you are about to read. Study each word and its meaning. Then answer the questions below. As you read the selection, notice how each vocabulary word is used.

domestic: not wild; tame
emerging: coming out
bleary: dull; blurred

escarpment: steep slope; cliff
endearing: inspiring affection
lethargic: slow; drowsy
subtlety: indirectness; secretness
precariousness: riskiness; uncertainty
decorous: in good taste; dignified
teeming: full; alive

1. Which word could describe your vision when you first wake up but are still tired?

2. Which word could describe a formal event at which everyone dressed elegantly and behaved beautifully?

3. Which word describes the action of people walking out of a meeting or conference?

4. Which word might describe the action of a turtle walking half awake across a sunny patio?

5. Which word might describe household animals like cats and dogs?

1. By late afternoon we have covered about 145 miles from Nairobi and are crossing into the Masai Mara National Reserve. Unlike the Serengeti to the south, the Mara is not a National Park and the Masai farmers are allowed to graze their flocks here. This mixture of the wild and the domestic, cows and sheep grazing alongside giraffe and elephant gives the Reserve a special, Noah's Ark quality....

2. When we reach our campsite by the banks of the Mara River, the tents have only just been erected and lavatories not yet dug nor beds erected. Patrick, the *maître de camp*, who has safaried with Hemingway, but still looks only 25, welcomes us, quickly introduces the staff of 13, makes us cups of tea and leaves us to look at the local river life. This consists of a colony of around 30 hippos puffing and wheezing like a lot of old men in a club after lunch. They apparently spend most of the day there, emerging at night to feed, and I'm told, wander through the camp. "It's perfectly all right so long as you stay in your tent," Martin advises, cheerfully.

3. We are on what is known as the "Out of Africa" safari—one up from the "Hemingway," which is one up from the "Kenya Under Canvas." This certainly isn't how I remember school camp. The tents are spacious. At the back, and under cover, there is a sort of dressing area, with a table and mirror, and a plastic toilet over a freshly dug hole. Beside the hole is a pile of earth, a small spade and a sign: "Hippos cover it up, will you do too." I have an old-fashioned bed, a solar-powered light and a rail for my clothes, and outside the roof of the tent extends over a washstand and a couple of canvas chairs, excellent for sitting out in before supper, and drinking a Scotch to the accompaniment of awfully rude noises from the river.

4. Dinner is served after a slight delay owing to the activity of baboons in the kitchen. Martin tells the story of one guest who felt a baboon against the side of his tent and whacked it with a heavy torch. It turned out to be a hippo, which charged off through the kitchen tent, which offered little resistance, and the hippo vanished into the bush with the kitchen wrapped around him.

5. 10:20 P.M.: The river is silent. A big moon casts a silvery light across the trees and banks of the river. A group of Masai from the local manyatta guard the camp, sitting by a wood fire and talking quietly. One of them, an elderly man with close-cropped gray hair, walks up and down between our tents and the river, ear-ringed, blanketed and carrying a spear. I feel very strongly that I am in a dream I once had, a long time ago.

6. Roars, splashes and hippo hoots mark the end of the night and I'm already awake when I hear the first human cry.

7. "Jambo!" comes from outside a nearby tent, followed by the sound of a door-flap being unzipped and bleary greetings from the occupants. It's 6 o'clock. There are no lie-ins on safari.

8. I'm Jambo-ed a minute or two later. A flask of tea, a plate of biscuits and milk in a china jug are set down by the bed and hot water poured into the washing bowl outside.

9. Dressed in my Colpro safari outfit, looking, and feeling, like a cut-price David Attenborough, I set out at 6:45, with the sun struggling to make an impression on a cloudy lifeless sky.

10. We make our way along the damp uneven track from the riverside toward the tall slope of the escarpment, passing zebra, impala and a grazing warthog. Warthogs—ugly, endearing creatures—live in the remains of anthills into which they insert themselves backwards. For some reason this makes me even more fond of them.

11. Six elephants, mighty ears flapping and trunks ripping at the croton bushes, move down the hill away from us. They only sleep about two hours a night, I'm told. Kalului, who has an extraordinary sixth sense about the presence of animals spots a lion couple, way in the distance. As we drive closer they turn out to be a somewhat battered male and a lethargic female. Neither seems to bat an eyelid at the circling presence of three vehicles and a clutch of cameras only yards away. The female, after washing and yawning, unhurriedly raises herself and the male immediately follows. He is limping. Lions spend about a week together mating, sometimes coupling as much as 880 times in 24 hours, but this affair looks to be over, if it ever began.

12. Meanwhile, in another episode of the Masai Mara soap opera, a male ostrich is doing his best to attract the ladies' attention. He cannot rely on subtlety as his legs turn pink during the mating season, so he goes for broke with an outrageous fan dance,

a wonderful spectacle of feather control, which does seem to have several female beaks turning in his direction.

13   In the midst of life we are in death. We pass Nubian vultures tearing away at the corpse of a zebra. These birds are known as the butchers, the only ones with necks and beaks powerful enough to open up a carcass. The coarse grass of the plain is littered with skulls, bones and skins, and the constant presence of vultures, eagles, buzzards and land scavengers like the jackals, with their sharp faces and big ears, is a reminder of the <u>precariousness</u> of life.

"A thousand feet below us the…Mara…[is] teeming with living things."

14   Our feeding is a little more <u>decorous</u>. We are treated to one of the set-pieces of an A and K safari—the "Out of Africa" breakfast. Whilst we have been ear-wigging lion couples, the staff from the camp have set up a long table, complete with fresh flowers and cut-glass butter-dishes, on the top of the Olololo escarpment. Eggs, bacon and sausage are sizzling on an open fire and the waiters are in dinner-jackets. The plain stretches away, flat and wide, between the escarpment walls of the Rift Valley, south toward Tanzania. A thousand feet below us the sunless Mara, which we know to be <u>teeming</u> with living things, looks gray and empty, except for a Second World War DC-3, which makes a wide, banking turn before settling down onto the airstrip, only a few hundred yards from where we watched the lions.

15   Later in the day gray clouds have filled the sky and the rain comes in, straight and heavy, putting an end to safari for that day.…

Starting Time   [   ]

Finishing Time   [   ]

Reading Time   [   ]

Reading Rate   [   ]

COMPREHENSION

Read the following questions and statements. For each one, put an X in the box before the option that contains the most complete or accurate answer.

1. The game reserve is about 145 miles from the city of
   - ☐ a. Capetown.
   - ☐ b. Nairobi.
   - ☐ c. Brazzaville.
   - ☐ d. Cairo.

2. The purpose of author Michael Palin's trip through this area is to
   - ☐ a. learn what primitive camping is like.
   - ☐ b. leave it behind him as quickly as possible.
   - ☐ c. see and photograph wild animals.
   - ☐ d. shoot wild animals.

3. The time frame for this episode is
   - ☐ a. one evening and the following day.
   - ☐ b. several days.
   - ☐ c. two weeks.
   - ☐ d. half a day.

4. A good statement of the main idea of this selection is the following:

 ☐ a. Most of the people who ran the safari didn't know what they were doing.

 ☐ b. Life during the safari was a combination of the natural and the sophisticated.

 ☐ c. Animals should be protected from humans who wish to harm them.

 ☐ d. The scenery in central Africa is some of the most beautiful in the world.

5. The local Masai are herders who raise

 ☐ a. corn.

 ☐ b. coffee and tea.

 ☐ c. cows and sheep.

 ☐ d. cotton and flax.

6. The activities of the ostriches and the vultures emphasize the contrast between

 ☐ a. fierce and timid animals.

 ☐ b. the young and the old.

 ☐ c. hunting for sport and hunting for food.

 ☐ d. the beginnings and the end of life.

7. Palin's reaction to the elaborate breakfast suggests that he finds it

 ☐ a. necessary.

 ☐ b. too expensive.

 ☐ c. somewhat silly.

 ☐ d. unfair to the poor people nearby.

8. The information in paragraphs 3 and 4 is presented in a tone that is meant to

 ☐ a. frighten.

 ☐ b. inform.

 ☐ c. anger.

 ☐ d. amuse.

9. As seen in this selection, Michael Palin appears to be a person who

 ☐ a. refuses to take anything seriously.

 ☐ b. has a keen eye for things going on around him.

 ☐ c. is concerned with animals more than people.

 ☐ d. is anxious to keep moving on his trip.

10. When Palin uses the metaphor "Masai Mara soap opera" in paragraph 12, he is referring to

 ☐ a. the fighting among the people on the safari.

 ☐ b. the romantic rituals among the animals.

 ☐ c. the anger of the Masai about foreigners entering their land.

 ☐ d. the dramatic music that can be heard on the radio.

Comprehension Skills Key

1. recalling specific facts
2. retaining concepts
3. organizing facts
4. understanding the main idea
5. drawing a conclusion
6. making a judgment
7. making an inference
8. recognizing tone
9. understanding characters
10. appreciating literary forms

VOCABULARY—PART TWO

Write the word that makes the most sense in each sentence.

domestic	emerging
bleary	escarpment
precariousness	

1. Palin woke up early in the morning, his eyes still _____ with sleep.

2. As he was _____ from his tent, he saw the sun just rising.

3. From the camp's position on the _____ , he could look down at the wide plains below.

4. As far as the eye could see were animals, both wild and _____ .

5. Walking along the steep-sided rim of the cliff, he realized the _____ of his position.

decorous   **teeming**
endearing   **lethargic**
subtlety

6. The crowded plains seemed to be

_____ with life.

7. Here were slow, _____ lions just

waking from a nap.

8. Here were huge giraffes, looking

_____ as they politely waited to

nibble the tops of trees.

9. The animals with the least _____

were the vultures, barging their way directly into

a crowd of dead or dying zebras.

10. To Palin the most _____ crea-

tures of all were the sweet, silly warthogs.

Comprehension   [   ]

Vocabulary   [   ]

UNDERSTANDING THROUGH WRITING

What do you think Michael Palin actually saw when he came out of his tent that morning? Use story details and write a short description.

_____

_____

_____

_____

_____

_____

_____

_____

BUILDING STUDY SKILLS

Read the following passage and answer the questions that follow it.

How to Remember, I

Here are three techniques to help you remember what you study.

1. Plan to Remember. This technique is obvious but it works. Tell yourself that you want to remember something and you will. For example, when you want to remember the name of someone you just met, say to yourself, "I'm going to listen carefully and repeat the name to be sure I have it."

2. Review the Material. Most forgetting occurs shortly after the learning has been done. More new material crowds out the information we've just studied, and we have trouble recalling it. The problem of too much information can be solved by reviewing. In fact, you can use previewing techniques when you review. Previewing again and recalling the questions you used at that time will give you enough of a review to help you remember.

3. Look for Principles. You cannot remember everything. Instead of looking at an assignment as vast quantities of material that must be remembered, generalize the subject into a few major ideas, or principles, that you can easily recall. You will find this technique especially effective in studying for quizzes and exams.

1. If you make an effort and _____ to

remember, you will.

2. Sometimes we forget what we've previously read

because new information _____

out the old.

3. A good way to review material is to use techniques

you learned in _____ .

4. Don't try to remember everything.

_____ the material into a few

major ideas that you can easily recall.

5. For example, when reviewing the selection you

just read, think about the two main time divisions:

the evening before and the actual day of the

_____ .

8

In Its Decay, Butte Sees a National Treasure

Timothy Egan

READING PURPOSE—
This selection describes a town in Montana that wants to be a tourist attraction for an unusual reason. Read to find out that reason.

VOCABULARY—PART ONE

All of these words are in the selection you are about to read. Study each word and its meaning. Then answer the questions below. As you read the selection, notice how each vocabulary word is used.

raucous: wild; disorderly

lynched: put to death without a trial

detritus: disintegrated material; remains

singular: unusual; noteworthy

encompass: include

deterred: stopped; prevented

aquifer: layer under the earth's surface that contains water

virtual: for all practical purposes; actual

legacy: something handed down

tenacious: stubborn; persistent

---

1. Which word could be an antonym for *ordinary*?

   _____

2. Which word might describe a noisy party?

   _____

3. Which word describes what the police officer did when he kept reporters from entering the crime scene?

   _____

4. Which word might describe someone who practices a golf swing for two hours until she gets it right?

   _____

5. Which word names a photograph that the first child in every generation of your family receives from his or her parents?

   _____

1   There is no doubt that what has happened over the last 120 years in this half-dead hill town just downslope from the Continental Divide has ranked among the more freakish, tragic and raucous episodes in American history.

2   Martial law was declared about a dozen times, with troops firing on striking miners. A labor leader was dragged from his home and lynched from a railroad trestle. Fire choked off a mine shaft in 1917, and 168 people suffocated nearly a half-mile underground. That's just the labor history.

3   In its industrial history, Butte was known as the richest hill on earth, the place that gave turn-of-the-century America most of its copper at a time when that was the crucial ingredient for a country newly linked by telephones and illuminated by electric light.

4   Finally, there is the account of what happened when the bill for it all came due. In 1985, the Federal government declared Butte and the surrounding region to be the biggest Superfund cleanup site in the country, nearly an entire county full of poisons and heavy metal, and still intertwined with living, breathing neighborhoods.

5   Now Butte is asking the official caretakers of the United States' natural and historical treasures to take up the question of whether this city and all its mine waste, slag heaps, Victorian homes, shuttered brothels, slumping hotels, skeletal mine shafts and related detritus should become one big national historic park.

6   Already, the National Park Service recognizes places like Lowell and New Bedford in Massachusetts as singular places worthy of the Park Service family. Textile mills are the draw in Lowell; New Bedford was once the center of the whaling world.

7   But Butte wants the concept of national historic park to encompass something altogether new. Typically, once a site is given an imprint from the Park Service, it receives a visitors center and Federal dollars and will usually be promoted as one of the nation's premier attractions. One of Butte's main distinctions—perhaps its central attraction, town leaders argue—is that it is one of the world's most visibly polluted and battered places.

8   Midway between Yellowstone National and Glacier National Parks would be a place to come see one of the worst industrial crimes against nature and a once-rich town struggling to live in its midst.

9   "Once you've done Yellowstone, then you come here to Butte to see how a Pittsburgh was just dropped in the middle of the Rocky Mountains," said Jack Lynch, the chief executive of the combined government of the City of Butte and Silver Bow County.

10   The mountains are scarred and tiered, still poked full of holes. The water that forms the headwaters of Clark Fork are laced with arsenic, manganese, lead, copper and zinc. Three generations of soot remain on the side of still-occupied workers' cottages.

11   At the center of Butte is the Berkeley Pit, a Grand Canyon of open-pit mining. The Pit is an 874-foot deep chasm filled with 26 billion gallons of contaminated water, an amount that grows by 3 million gallons a day as ground water moves into the old open mine and becomes part of the toxic stew.

12   Two years ago, more than 300 snow geese had the misfortune of landing in The Pit, mistaking its water for a normal lake at night. The acid corroded the birds' stomachs and killed them.

13   But Butte is as tough a town as the West has ever produced, and none of these seeming handicaps has deterred the people who live here from trying to show off this peculiar American hybrid. They propose covering as much of the waste and mine tailings as possible—until they are no longer an immediate threat to health or the environment—then incorporating the rest of the waste into the grand historic park. There is plenty of in-state opposition to the plan by people who say the park plan may let the polluters off the hook.

14   Mr. Lynch said the park would have many attractions. Many of its ornate, custom-designed buildings and homes, now largely abandoned, have been protected since 1962, when Butte was designated a National Historic Landmark.

15   "We have The Pit," Mr. Lynch said. "We have architecture. We have the only dead aquifer in the United States, I believe. We went from the wrecking ball to the mothball because we realize all of this has value."…

16   Butte was the ultimate company town, owned by the Anaconda Copper Company and its later corporate incarnations. And Montana was a virtual company state at the turn of the century. The

company owned the water and power supply, the biggest timber mills, most politicians and every newspaper in the state but one.

17　　One legacy of the copper kings who ran Butte is that the town still looks for dependence on some big corporate or government entity, Mr. Lynch said. But if the Park Service accepts Butte as a national historic park, the plan would be to have most of the town continue to run itself, he said, with minimal Park Service staffing.

18　　"I guess you would call it a working museum, with shops, homes, cleanup sites all going about their business under the imprint of a big national park," Mr. Lynch said.

19　　Butte has endured its share of ridicule since it began to promote itself as a national treasure, but townspeople do not seem bothered.

20　　"People here are tenacious," Mr. Lynch said, sitting in his office in a 1910 building with marble columns and copper doors. "They never say die in Butte."

21　　Judging by the midweek traffic in August, it is hard to imagine hordes of people detouring off the road to Yellowstone to picnic next to heaps of black mine waste. At the place where 168 miners were killed by a fire, not a single car came to visit on a recent afternoon.

22　　And the old company town still faces one looming deadline. Sometime in the next 25 years, The Pit is expected to reach "critical water level," the point at which the soup of pollutants would start to trickle into wells, streams and drinking water. Butte plans to have a pump running by then but has not figured out where the water would go or where it would be treated.

"'We have the pit,' Mr. Lynch said. 'We have architecture…. We went from the wrecking ball to the mothball because we realize all of this has value.'"

23　　But the very thing that could ultimately destroy Butte remains its biggest draw. People do detour off Interstate 90 to view the half-empty hill where much of old downtown Butte was swallowed by The Pit.

24　　They may come for the same reason that people slow to look at car wrecks but that is of no concern to Butte. What matters is that people are still curious.

Starting Time	
Finishing Time	
Reading Time	
Reading Rate	

COMPREHENSION

Read the following questions and statements. For each one, put an X in the box before the option that contains the most complete or accurate answer.

1. The city of Butte is situated
   - ☐ a. near the Pacific coast.
   - ☐ b. in the Rio Grande Valley.
   - ☐ c. on the Great Plains.
   - ☐ d. near two national parks.

2. The article tells of a struggle between
   - ☐ a. the city and its polluters.
   - ☐ b. the city and the federal government.
   - ☐ c. the older residents and the people who have just moved in.
   - ☐ d. the working class citizens and the company owners.

3. The purpose of this selection is to
   - ☐ a. tell a story in time order.
   - ☐ b. give information.
   - ☐ c. describe a scenic location.
   - ☐ d. persuade the government to give the city of Butte what it wants.

4. What is Butte's main argument for becoming a national historic park?
   - ☐ a. It was an important settlement in the Wild West.
   - ☐ b. It is one of the largest cities in Montana.
   - ☐ c. It is an example of what happens when industrial pollution is uncontrolled.
   - ☐ d. It has a number of noteworthy Victorian houses.

5. Compared with its earlier days, Butte
   - ☐ a. is just as lively as it ever was.
   - ☐ b. is quieter than it used to be.
   - ☐ c. remains a good place to bring up a family.
   - ☐ d. is more polluted now than twenty years ago.

6. The author's opinion seems to be that
   - ☐ a. some visitors would be interested in some of Butte's sites.
   - ☐ b. the national historic park would be a great success.
   - ☐ c. the national historic park would be a total failure.
   - ☐ d. other cities would do well to come up with plans similar to Butte's.

7. The reason that the park plan may let polluters off the hook is that
   - ☐ a. they would be free to pollute other nearby areas.
   - ☐ b. they would no longer have to clean up the entire mess.
   - ☐ c. visitors' money would pay to clean up the area.
   - ☐ d. the government would use the polluted sites for new experiments.

8. In talking about the situation in Butte, the tone the writer uses is
   - ☐ a. bitter.
   - ☐ b. mocking.
   - ☐ c. matter-of-fact.
   - ☐ d. humorous.

9. The people of Butte
   - ☐ a. are determined to get what they want.
   - ☐ b. fear that the rest of the country would be jealous of their fame.
   - ☐ c. are capable of laughing at themselves.
   - ☐ d. still believe they are living in a frontier town.

10. In discussing the situation in Butte, the author uses
    - ☐ a. only facts from history.
    - ☐ b. a lot of exaggeration.
    - ☐ c. only facts from the present.
    - ☐ d. a combination of historical and current facts.

Comprehension Skills Key

1. recalling specific facts
2. retaining concepts
3. organizing facts
4. understanding the main idea
5. drawing a conclusion
6. making a judgment
7. making an inference
8. recognizing tone
9. understanding characters
10. appreciating literary forms

VOCABULARY—PART TWO

Write the word that makes the most sense in each sentence.

detritus	singular
deterred	aquifer
legacy	

1. Butte's _____ is so polluted that the people can no longer use water from it.

2. There is _____ all over the city from falling-apart buildings and factories.

3. The _____ of its wild, uncontrolled days remains with the city generations later.

4. Yet those "bad old days" have not _____ Butte from believing it is something special.

5. In fact, the people have a _____ plan for saving their city, so unusual that it might just work.

encompass   raucous
lynched   tenacious
virtual

6. The citizens of Butte know people have been

    _____ in their city for crimes

    they didn't commit.

7. They know that noisy dance halls and

    _____ saloons used to line the

    main street.

8. The stories the old-timers tell

    _____ all types of lawlessness

    and corruption.

9. No doubt about it, Butte was a

    _____ hell hole for much of its

    history.

10. But the citizens are _____ : they

    will hold fast until they get the recognition they

    believe they deserve.

Comprehension [   ]

Vocabulary [   ]

UNDERSTANDING THROUGH WRITING

Do you think the government should make Butte a national historic town? Why or why not? Write your answer and a short explanation of your reasons for it.

_____

_____

_____

_____

_____

_____

_____

_____

_____

_____

_____

BUILDING STUDY SKILLS

Read the following passage and answer the questions that follow it.

Signs and Signals

Well-written texts contain many *signs* that are meant to guide the reader. Signs are different from *signals*, which we will discuss later.

For our purposes, signs refer to the use of numbers and letters to point out the value or the sequence of thoughts. Perhaps the most commonly recognized reading signs are the numbers 1, 2, 3, and so on. Their roles as indicators of worth or order are readily apparent to most readers. Sometimes they are followed by another sign: "There are *three* major causes of baldness." Upon seeing the word *three*, the reader knows that numbers will soon follow.

Letters are often used in the same way as numbers. A, B, and C or a, b, and c appear consistently throughout texts to guide the reader.

Integral words in the text can also work as signs. The words *one, two,* and *three,* or *first, second,* and *third* have value and importance to the reader, even though they do not stand out in the text the way alphanumeric signs do.

Still other signs are the phrases *in the first place, in the second place,* and so on. They also serve to inform the reader that numbering is taking place, though the reader may be only partially aware of that process. But it is essential that such phrases be in some way numbered by the reader if the ideas they list are to have the significance the author intended.

Signs are more likely to appear in certain places in a chapter. Often they are used at the beginning to list the important elements to be covered.

Another place to look for signs is at the end of a chapter or section. There they are used as a summary listing of important elements discussed in the preceding material.

1. Signs refer to the use of numbers and

    _____ to point out important

    ideas.

2. Also used as signs are words and phrases. For

    example, we may see the word *fourth* used instead

    of the number _____ .

3. In the second paragraph in the article on Butte,

    there are three facts about its history that could

    have been given _____ .

4. Signs are often found at the _____

    of the chapter, listing important things to come.

5. Signs are also found at the end of the chapter

    where they are used to list _____

    of important ideas.

9

Letter from France

Maya Angelou

READING PURPOSE—
In this selection, writer and actor Maya Angelou has a somewhat surprising reaction to traveling through France. As you read, see if you can predict what her final reaction will be.

VOCABULARY—PART ONE

All of these words are in the selection you are about to read. Study each word and its meaning. Then answer the questions below. As you read the selection, notice how each vocabulary word is used.

propensity: tendency

desultorily: in an aimless or unplanned method

intrepid: fearless

dispel: get rid of; drive away

chagrin: embarrassment

indelible: not erasable

atrophying: wasting away from lack of use

improbable: questionable; not very likely

cajoled: coaxed; wheedled

solace: comfort; relief

1. Which word might describe your feelings if you discovered that you had put on one brown and one black shoe this morning?

2. Which word could describe a firefighter who rushes into a burning building to save a child?

3. Which word describes ink that remains permanently on a paper?

4. Which word might you use to describe the plot of a TV sitcom episode that doesn't seem very true to life?

5. Which word tells what a can of bug spray might do to a colony of ants?

1   From the window of my cottage in the Berkeley Hills, I watched the sun glinting on the windshields of cars crossing the Golden Gate Bridge and the traffic helicopter hovering like a metal dragonfly over the silver Bay Bridge. Everybody was going someplace. Since I had just turned in my latest book to my editor, I didn't think anyone deserved a trip more than I.

2   During this time, I had a houseguest (I'll call him Paul Du Feu) who was a world traveler. We had spent many nights in front of my fireplace laughing together at his experiences in the Canadian forests, or in living rough on the beaches of Spain, or selling cars in Germany. He dared adventure and always landed on his feet. Admitting my own lack of daring and my propensity to stay on the beaten path, I thought he would make the ideal traveling companion. He agreed. And since he had just turned in a finished manuscript, he said he, too, merited a vacation.

3   The TWA Red Eye Special (leaving San Francisco at 10:00 P.M. and arriving New York at 6:00 A.M.) was just what I expected it to be. Although the service was first class, the jet lag and cocktails at 37,000 feet made me a perfect "before" model for an eyewash advertisement. New York City at dawn is as nice as it's likely to be, so from the air I watched the skyscrapers through rose-colored eyes and projected myself toward the evening transatlantic flight.

4   The next morning, from London's Heathrow Airport (where all but tourists respect the taxi queues), we traveled to South London where friends had lent us a newly renovated Victorian house. The bay windows looked out over Wandsworth Common, and the backyard reminded me of the garden I left in California. Mornings I slept late, then worked desultorily among the string beans while Paul raked casually around the tomatoes. At noon, we walked to the corner pub and drank our share of good lukewarm beer, appropriately called "bitter."

5   After a few weeks, I had to admit that my life had not qualitatively changed. I had simply changed locale. True, London's streets were clean and colorful, but so are Berkeley's. Admittedly, shop attendants and waitresses were courteous, but then so are they in the Bay Area. *The Daily Mail* livened my morning tea, but the *San Francisco Chronicle* did the same for my coffee.

6   Obviously, it was time to move on to more exotic places.

7   James Baldwin had invited me many times to come to see his house in the south of France. He has long been my friend, brother, and favorite writer. Since I was so near, since London was reminding me more and more of northern California, since Paul was beginning to show just an edge of edginess, I suggested that we tear ourselves loose and bound over to southern France. He agreed readily.

8   We packed the hardly used gardening tools, put the borrowed house in order, and telephoned BEA for reservations to Nice. When we were told the ticket rates (seventy-eight pounds sterling each, one way, London-Nice) we were nearly shocked into remaining in London. But Paul, the intrepid adventurer, suggested buying a car, an old used car, preferably a retired post-office van ("one driver, whose use of it was mostly in parking along shady streets"). Fortunately, a friend had an Austin Mini Countryman he needed to rid himself of. The car was in "excellent condition," only nine years old, and had spent most of those years "parked along shady streets."

9   We drove aboard the British Sea Link Ferry in New Haven at 10:00 P.M., and at midnight, as the ship pulled out into the channel, we toasted each other in the well-appointed dining room with a solid French wine that was nearly as good as Gallo's Hearty Burgundy.

10   Dawn in Dieppe. Three times the morning fog lifted for two seconds as I picked the car's way through the town's narrow cobbled streets and out onto a gray highway. An arrow promised Rouen and, since Paul was sleeping off our shipboard celebration, I had no choice but to trust the promise. A pale sun rose on the Normandy countryside, and it was a dreary setting for an Ingmar Bergman film. But as the light strengthened, the fertility of the land was more evident. Thatched cottages and prosperous farmhouses sat back from the highway in San Joaquin Valley green. I tried to people the landscape with conquering Normans from old history books or allied troops from World War II, but the tiny car wrestled along the road like a hooked trout, and before I could let my attention wander, I had driven through Rouen and reached the outskirts of a fairly large town.

11   Paul awoke, ashamed that he had slept through the hard part of the drive. I did nothing to dispel his chagrin except to quote Thomas Wolfe on man:

12 He lived and he was here! He needed speech to ask for bread and he had Christ! He needed songs to sing in battle and he had Homer! He wove the robes of Solomon! He needed a temple to propitiate his God and he made Chartres!

13 "Are we in Chartres?"

14 "Oui."

"We sat at a sidewalk restaurant off a cobbled square and had our first *petit pain* and *café au lait*."

15 We sat at a sidewalk restaurant off a cobbled square and had our first *petit pain* and *café au lait*. The wonders of fresh bread, sweet butter, and hot coffee were partly lost on me since I was still trying to unfold my six-foot frame from the pattern the small car was molding me into. Paul popped under the wheel and guided the car back to the highway. Over the rooftops I spied the spires of the cathedral called by Rodin the "Acropolis of France." Once back on the road, I mentally ticked off Chartres. It has been done.

16 We hurtled, devil-may-care, through rural France at the car's top speed of 50 mph. By one o'clock, we stormed into Bourges. The Gothic 15th-century town didn't warm under the bright sunlight, and visions of medieval barbarity sugar-plummed in my head. Since we carried no *Guide Michelin* or gourmet's map, we chose the first restaurant we saw and had a fine meal. The menu and the name of the establishment are forgotten, but the local Sancerre wine left an <u>indelible</u> and good memory.

17 My dashing companion jangled the car keys and said no to another bottle of the local vintage. Over the steep roofs, I think I caught sight of a corner of the famous Bourges cathedral. As we tootled to the highway, I checked off Bourges. It was done.

18 The meadows and pastures unfolded slowly out the Austin's sliding windows in nearly the same rhythm that my legs, shoulders, and arms were <u>atrophying</u> within the car. By five-thirty we drove into Roanne, and I thought it would be easier to sleep where I was than to demand the <u>improbable</u> of my aching body.

19 We moved into the fading but elegant Hotel Centrale as if we planned to stay for a month. Paul and a too-thin bellboy carried our six large bags and a box of books into the hotel's strong room, since one of the car doors refused to lock securely. A long steamy bath <u>cajoled</u> my muscles into resuming their work, and by nine o'clock we followed the hotel manager's directions to the Restaurant Alsace-Lorraine. We ate a well-prepared and abundantly served dinner and walked the quiet dark streets back to the hotel.

20 Morning found us pleated back into the car and on the highway. Lyons flew by in a haze of pink hill chateaux[1] and modern high-rise buildings....

21 We drove, finally, to Cannes and up the twisting roads to St. Paul. Near midnight we parked our pressure cooker at the edge of a tiny square and saw men in short sleeves playing *boule* under the lights. The elegant Colombe d'Or restaurant, where Picasso, Yves Montand, Simone Signoret, and Baldwin were known to "lift a few," faced the square. We ordered drinks at a lesser known bistro nearby and telephoned Jimmy. In minutes he strode into the square, jacket flung casually across his shoulders, a wide grin across his face. He is a celebrity. Tourists and natives alike recognized him, and he returned their salutes warmly—then gave me a family embrace. He said he'd guide us to his house.

22 The villa suits a great writer and especially James Baldwin. It is glamorous. Baldwin is glamorous. It is romantic. The romance of Baldwin lies in the fact that his warmth makes us nearly forget that he is a giant. And the house is comfortable to be near.

23 Yet, with the exception of a gay reunion with my friend, the destination was to prove anticlimactic. My soreness resisted the <u>solace</u> of a bed. The

---

[1]*chateaux:* plural of *chateau*, a large French country house

smells of old bread, melting butter, and stale wine from the car clung to the lining of my nostrils and made it difficult for me to appreciate the talents of Baldwin's highly praised cook.

24   We sat under a grapevine-laced arbor that has its counterpart on a ranch in Sonoma owned by a winegrowing friend. The company's conversation dealt with Life, Taxes, Politics, Love, and the Arts. The same subjects we had all discussed in Paris, London, New York, and Berkeley.

25   Outside the walled villa, the streets of St. Paul, LaColle, Cagnes, and Cannes resembled Macy's toy department during the Christmas season. Cars crawled 5 mph along the undoubtedly beautiful corniche,[2] and pedestrians more anxious for their tans than in staying whole, wedged between bumpers on their way to the sea. It was a sunny Sunday afternoon in Sausalito, which had been leased to beauty-hungry tourists from Los Angeles.

26   "How long do you want to stay?"

27   I hoped I was reading Paul correctly. "I'm ready to head north," I answered.

28   He smiled. "We'll leave at dawn."

29   That suited me.

30   I said good-bye to my friends in St. Paul and spent the next day and the next waving fond adieus to the familiar lay-bys. A day later, I was gathering fresh zucchini, eggplant, and onions from my backyard in Berkeley. I made a *ratatouille provençale*.[3]

Starting Time	
Finishing Time	
Reading Time	
Reading Rate	

---

[2]*corniche:* winding road cut into the side of a cliff along a coast
[3]*ratatouille provençale:* cold vegetable dish originally developed in the south of France

COMPREHENSION

Read the following questions and statements. For each one, put an X in the box before the option that contains the most complete or accurate answer.

1. The author found the Austin car
   - ☐ a. unattractive.
   - ☐ c. unpredictable.
   - ☐ b. uncomfortable.
   - ☐ d. unmanageable.

2. During her trip, the author
   - ☐ a. stayed in a number of cities.
   - ☐ b. spent most of her time with James Baldwin.
   - ☐ c. visited England, France, and Germany.
   - ☐ d. did not get along well with her traveling companion.

3. The author stayed in South London for
   - ☐ a. one night.
   - ☐ c. several weeks.
   - ☐ b. three nights.
   - ☐ d. six months.

4. The author gradually came to realize that
   - ☐ a. there is high adventure on the open road.
   - ☐ b. writers are very special people.
   - ☐ c. Europeans are very sophisticated.
   - ☐ d. there is no place like home.

5. The author's favorite place to be is
   - ☐ a. South London.
   - ☐ b. Berkeley, California.
   - ☐ c. Rouen, France.
   - ☐ d. New York City.

6. The author's decision to go on vacation seems
   - ☐ a. impractical.
   - ☐ b. comical.
   - ☐ c. sound.
   - ☐ d. poorly thought out.

7. The Red Eye Special
   - ☐ a. offers second-rate service.
   - ☐ b. is an unpopular flight.
   - ☐ c. is never on time.
   - ☐ d. seems named for the time it flies.

8. The author's mood during her travels abroad seems
   - ☐ a. restless.
   - ☐ c. content.
   - ☐ b. confused.
   - ☐ d. bitter.

60

9. The author may be considered
   ☐ a. a daring traveler.
   ☐ b. someone who doesn't like being told what to do.
   ☐ c. a person who feels more comfortable at home.
   ☐ d. a woman in love.

10. When the author describes a traffic helicopter looking "like a metal dragonfly," she is using
    ☐ a. a literal description.   ☐ c. a metaphor.
    ☐ b. a simile.   ☐ d. personification.

Comprehension Skills Key

1. recalling specific facts
2. retaining concepts
3. organizing facts
4. understanding the main idea
5. drawing a conclusion
6. making a judgment
7. making an inference
8. recognizing tone
9. understanding characters
10. appreciating literary forms

VOCABULARY—PART TWO

Write the word that makes the most sense in each sentence.

intrepid   **dispel**
indelible   **cajoled**
solace

1. Maya Angelou has _____ memories of that trip through France, images that will stay in her mind forever.

2. Through flattery and coaxing, she had _____ her friend Paul into coming with her.

3. One purpose of taking an exciting trip was to _____ the boredom of the last few months.

4. Paul was a(n) _____ traveler, one who would never turn away from a scary situation.

5. Maya took _____ in the fact that he would be there to protect her if needed.

chagrin   **propensity**
desultorily   **atrophying**
improbable

6. Maya was restless and had a(n) _____ for moving from place to place.

7. She and Paul drove through France _____ , never sure where they would be the next day.

8. It was _____ that Maya would enjoy the long rides, crammed as she was into a small car.

9. She was sure that one of her legs was _____ from being stuck in the same position for so long.

10. Since it was she who had pushed for the trip, it was with some _____ that she told Paul she wanted to return home.

Comprehension [ ]

Vocabulary [ ]

UNDERSTANDING THROUGH WRITING

What could Maya Angelou have done to make her trip more enjoyable? Write some suggestions that you think could have helped her have a better time.

_____

_____

_____

_____

_____

_____

_____

BUILDING STUDY SKILLS

Read the following passage and answer the questions that follow it.

Forward Signals

Signals are useful guides for the reader, even though they are not as apparent as signs. The first types of signals that we are going to look at are called Forward Signals.

Forward Signals indicate that more of the same is coming and that the reader should continue forward. The most common Forward Signals are *and, more, moreover, more than that, furthermore, also,* and *likewise.*

The most frequently used word in that group is *and.* It is a forward signal indicating that another item of equal importance will follow or that the items are parts of a series. It tells you that you will not be faced with an opposing or reversing thought—you can go right on for more of the same.

The signals *more, moreover, more than that,* and *furthermore* all indicate that new and even stronger thoughts are coming up: "She's clever all right; *more than that,* she's a genius." It is plain how such signals strengthen and add depth to the original idea.

The signal *likewise* means "in the same manner." *Also* indicates that statements of ideas quite similar to those that have preceded are about to follow: "Along with signs, authors *also* use signals."

Signals are unlike signs in many ways. Signs are usually placed above or in front of numbered material. Signals, on the other hand, are words or phrases, and they are woven into the text. They are not set apart from the rest of the copy. For that reason, they are not as easy to spot as signs, and they therefore require the reader to be alert for their appearance and function.

1. Other words that _____ the reader are called signals.

2. Signals are more _____ to find than signs because they do not stand out from the rest of the text.

3. Forward Signals tell the reader to _____ .

4. In the sentence "The wonders of fresh bread, sweet butter, and hot coffee were partly lost on me," the word *and* indicates that the items are parts of a _____ .

5. In the sentence "Obviously, it was time to move on to more exotic places," the signal word *more* tells the reader that the information to follow will add _____ to the original idea.

10

Moscow on the Make

Bill Powell and Owen Matthews

READING PURPOSE—
In the years before Communist control of Russia ended in the early 1990s, Moscow was a much different city from what it is today. Read this selection to see the differences between Moscow then and Moscow now.

VOCABULARY—PART ONE

All of these words are in the selection you are about to read. Study each word and its meaning. Then answer the questions below. As you read the selection, notice how each vocabulary word is used.

revelers: people having a good time

demise: death; end

decadence: moral decay

enticingly: attractively; appealingly

manic: wild, uncontrolled excitement

capital: money

oligarchs: people of the ruling class

massive: huge; enormous

revitalization: a bringing to life again

humiliation: shame; embarrassment

---

1. Which word could you use in describing a sixty-foot-tall statue?

_____

2. Which word names something that is needed to finance any building project?

_____

3. Which word could describe people celebrating on New Year's Eve?

_____

4. Which word could be an antonym for *peasants*?

_____

5. Which word is a synonym for *rebirth*?

_____

1 It's 3 A.M. on a warm summer night, and scores of young revelers pour onto a riverbank from a clutch of neighboring nightclubs. Some of the kids are drunk; some are stoned; some flirt; some just lie back and look at the night sky. They are relaxed, casual. The setting could be any European capital. But this is a riverbank called Raushskaya, just across from Red Square, the center and soul of the city of Moscow.

2 During the decades of communism, Moscow meant gray, lifeless, oppression; it meant waiting in long lines for stores with empty shelves; it meant tapped telephones and KGB informants. It seemed like a city that did everything it could to live up to being the capital of the Evil Empire. Since communism's demise six years ago, it has come to conjure up very different images: mob hits, murdered businessmen, a Parliament building shelled by Russia's own army; filthy-rich robber barons partying and spending wildly.

3 Those images are real enough. There is an edge—a wildness and a decadence—to life in Moscow at the end of the 20th century. But the images are also incomplete—and not very revealing about the sort of place Russia's capital has become. They conflict with scenes like the one on the embankment, images that are enticingly hopeful about a country struggling to reinvent itself.

4 Next month Moscow and its ambitious mayor, Yuri Luzhkov, are going to throw a huge party. Pavarotti will sing in Red Square, and James Brown will be there, too. For the first time since the 1980 Olympics, old buildings are being sandblasted to reveal an elegance jarringly at odds with the city's dreary image. The occasion of the $40 million blowout is the 850th anniversary of the city's founding. But if the number doesn't seem much more significant than 849 or 851, it doesn't mean there isn't cause for celebration…. The mayor's stated reason for inviting the world to his city…is, he says, to celebrate Moscow's emergence as a "normal, civilized capital."

5 That's a bit premature. But what separates Moscow from the rest of Russia today is the *hope* that it can be normal, particularly among the young, for whom the cold war is just another chapter in a history book. As Julia Koroleva, a 30-year-old who left for Los Angeles in 1991 and returned this year to work in a public-relations firm, puts it, "There's something new in the air here…a sense that all the past has really been shed, that we are no longer crippled by the heavy weight our parents carried."

6 Russia's capital today bursts with as much manic capitalistic energy as Tokyo or New York or London. It's no secret that there is fabulous wealth in the New Moscow; six of the world's 500 richest people live there, according to *Forbes*. More important, the massive capital flight that has plagued Russia since 1991 is reversing. Switzerland last year became the leading foreign investor in Russia, and that only confirmed the obvious: a lot of Russian money is coming home. The reason for that is simple. In Moscow, as in any other center of capitalism, the making of money attracts more money. In the first six months of this year, Moscow's stock market doubled in value, and that followed a 130 percent gain in 1996. The average daily trading volume has risen from $2.3 million to $43.3 million in just two years.

7 Not just speculators and oligarchs are reaping the dividends. Aleksandr K, 25, is one of a growing number of young professionals doing well—and doing so within the law. (Concerned about shakedowns, he doesn't want his name revealed.) He is a broker for a major Russian securities company, earns $60,000 a year, vacations in Europe with his young wife, and is saving to buy an apartment in the center of town. "People of my age with brains don't have to go into criminal, shady business," he says. "There's a normal career ladder now, which you climb if you are smart, not because you have [Communist] Party connections or because you killed someone."

8 Moscow is now the only city in Russia with a rapidly growing middle class. Car ownership in Moscow is up to more than 3 million from 700,000 in 1991. Mayor Luzhkov has used the city's relatively flush tax rolls to fund a massive public-works binge. The city's signature project is the Christ the Savior Cathedral. A 15-story marble edifice, it is topped with a giant onion dome made with 110 pounds of solid gold. It sits on the same site as the original Christ the Savior Church, which Stalin dynamited in 1931. The Manezh Square next to the Kremlin has been transformed into an underground shopping mall. The once dilapidated facades of Tverskaya, the city's main street, have turned into a golden mile of expensive, Western-style stores and five-star hotels. Donald Trump is shopping for property near Red Square.

9   But the city's <u>revitalization</u> has also bred a kind of decadence that dwarfs that of any other European capital. Where there were fewer than 10 nightclubs three years ago, there are now more than 300, and the number is rising steadily. At the crowded Hungry Duck, bartenders serve four free shots of tequila for every one ordered; by midnight, people are dancing topless on the bar. At the Up and Down Club, "businessmen" may pay $350 just to get in, then choose from among stunning women, some of whom command $500 an hour. At the Moscow Palace of Youth, 1,000 rave-happy youngsters dance till 6 in the morning to pumping techno in a giant Brezhnev-era auditorium built for the Young Communist League. In the clubs, everything from marijuana to Ecstasy is available.

"What separates Moscow from the rest of Russia today is the hope that it can be normal."

10   Although the rate of violent crime has begun to dip, the mafia remains an obnoxiously visible force, ever-present just behind the tinted windows of the Mercedes that just drove past. Crime doesn't seem like a journalistic cliché when you step out of a theater during the Moscow Film Festival, round a corner and walk into the immediate aftermath of a double homicide. Most businesses in Moscow continue to pay protection money. They have what's known as a mafia *krysha*, or "roof."…

11   Still, for all its painfully sharp edges, Moscow is the only place in Russia where the promise of the post-communist revolution is at all visible. The youngsters on the embankment every weekend aren't mafiosi, nor are they the 'golden youth" generation of children of Communist Party apparatchiks.[1] They are ordinary middle-class

---

[1]*apparatchiks:* members of the political power structure

youngsters enjoying the first breath of Moscow's new-found prosperity. They buy rollerblades and laptop computers. They order out for pizza. They go to a Moscow club after work and have a few beers. They will, no doubt, snap up the Russian version of London's weekly entertainment-and-arts guide *Time Out* when it's unveiled this fall.

12   In most places these things are unremarkable. Not here. The word in Russian is *normalnost*—"normalcy." The young people in Moscow have it today in a way their parents could not ever imagine, and many are beginning to believe things will only get better. "Daily life is not a <u>humiliation</u> anymore" is how Julia Koroleva, the 30-year-old returnee, puts it. There is enormous hope in that phrase. Hope enough, in fact, to justify one hell of an anniversary party.

Starting Time	
Finishing Time	
Reading Time	
Reading Rate	

COMPREHENSION

Read the following questions and statements. For each one, put an X in the box before the option that contains the most complete or accurate answer.

1. The mayor of Moscow was throwing a party for the city's
   - ☐ a. 850th anniversary.
   - ☐ b. 250th anniversary.
   - ☐ c. 1,000th anniversary.
   - ☐ d. 100th anniversary.

2. Life for young people in Moscow is now basically
   - ☐ a. enjoyable.
   - ☐ b. hard.
   - ☐ c. frustrating.
   - ☐ d. unchanged from before.

3. The writers of this story make their points by
   - ☐ a. alternating descriptions of Moscow's past and Moscow's present.
   - ☐ b. telling about the life of one young Moscow citizen.
   - ☐ c. giving many examples of what life in Moscow is like now.
   - ☐ d. starting in the present and then going to a flashback.

4. A Moscow citizen returning after twenty years would find the city
   - ☐ a. as dull and gray as ever.
   - ☐ b. a virtual paradise, with nearly all its problems solved.
   - ☐ c. a place with problems but with a lot of excitement and optimism too.
   - ☐ d. completely rebuilt.

5. The authors think that most of their readers see current-day Moscow as
   - ☐ a. a place where young people run wild.
   - ☐ b. filled with crime and corruption.
   - ☐ c. a city with a steadily growing population.
   - ☐ d. a place where old people are ignored.

6. Mayor Luzhkov's plan for improving the city is to
   - ☐ a. invite exiles to return home.
   - ☐ b. throw parties.
   - ☐ c. arrest wrongdoers.
   - ☐ d. build and restore.

7. In paragraph 7, Aleksandr K is worried about a "shakedown" by
   - ☐ a. the police.
   - ☐ b. the mafia.
   - ☐ c. his competitors.
   - ☐ d. his company.

8. In paragraph 5, the tone that Julia Koroleva uses in describing Moscow is
   - ☐ a. sad.
   - ☐ b. angry.
   - ☐ c. hopeful.
   - ☐ d. concerned.

9. Aleksandr K can best be called
   - ☐ a. ambitious.
   - ☐ b. corrupt.
   - ☐ c. struggling to make ends meet.
   - ☐ d. unconcerned about his fellow citizens.

10. When the writers say that Moscow "bursts with as much…energy as Tokyo or New York," they are using
    - ☐ a. a simile.
    - ☐ b. a metaphor.
    - ☐ c. a realistic comparison.
    - ☐ d. personification.

Comprehension Skills Key

1. recalling specific facts
2. retaining concepts
3. organizing facts
4. understanding the main idea
5. drawing a conclusion
6. making a judgment
7. making an inference
8. recognizing tone
9. understanding characters
10. appreciating literary forms

VOCABULARY—PART TWO

Write the word that makes the most sense in each sentence.

demise	**capital**
massive	**revitalization**
humiliation	

1. For many years people from Moscow were embarrassed by their city and felt _____ in talking about it.

2. However, the _____ of communism brought about the birth of a better society.

3. Since the problems were so huge, _____ amounts of money were spent on trying to solve them.

4. This _____ came from legal and illegal financial sources.

5. A city on the verge of death experienced a great _____ .

decadence	**enticingly**
manic	**oligarchs**
revelers	

6. During city celebrations, the _____ sometimes go a little crazy.

7. Some people become _____ and run wild in the streets.

8. Many people dress _____ to attract the opposite sex.

9. The _____ would like to control the working-class people, but they cannot.

10. These people believe the celebrations are signs of _____ rather than clean, innocent fun.

Comprehension	☐
Vocabulary	☐

UNDERSTANDING THROUGH WRITING

Pretend you are a young student living in Moscow. Write a letter to a friend in America telling what you like about your city. Use specifics from the story to support what you say.

_____

_____

_____

_____

_____

_____

_____

_____

_____

_____

_____

_____

BUILDING STUDY SKILLS

Read the following passage and answer the questions that follow it.

Summary Signals

We have already seen some signals that appear in the text to encourage the reader to move forward because more ideas of the same kind are coming. As you will recall, they are called Forward Signals.

Other signals that also urge the reader forward are called Summary Signals. They are also Forward Signals, but we put them in their own group because the job they do is much more specific. They signal not only that the thought is going on, but also that a new idea is being introduced. The new idea will be one of summary or consequence.

Words such as *thus, therefore, consequently,* and *accordingly* tell the reader that the author is not only advancing the first thought but is also introducing an added one. That added idea will wrap up what has already been said or will reveal the result of earlier ideas. The reader, alerted by the signal words to the new idea, is made aware that the author has been leading up to a synthesis of the original and the new ideas. At that point, the writer will, ideally, pause and summarize the complete thought and show the result or effect it has produced.

In textbooks especially, Summary Signals identify ideas and concepts the author feels are of great importance. Frequently, they appear at the beginning of statements that summarize the writer's presentation. Summary Signals do not occur as often in less formal texts.

1. Summary Signals are a special kind of Forward Signal, because they _____ a new idea.

2. That added idea will often _____ what has already been said.

3. The Summary Signal alerts the reader that the author is leading up to a _____ of the original and the new ideas.

4. Suppose that in paragraph 7 of "Moscow on the Make," the order of the last two sentences was reversed. Then a Summary Signal like *therefore* would come just before the _____.

5. In _____ especially, Summary Signals can introduce important conclusions by the author.

TOPIC REVIEW
React to Topic 2

Respond to one or more of these questions as your instructor directs.

1. Butte and Moscow are alike in that both cities have had big problems in the past. In what other ways are they alike? In what ways are they different? Make a list of at least three similarities and three differences between the two cities.

_____

_____

_____

_____

_____

2. There are strong differences between the landscapes that Michael Palin and Maya Angelou describe. Review "Into the Kenyan Game Reserve" and "Letter from France," making notes on the differences. Then write a paragraph or two explaining what they are. Include at least three differences in your writing.

_____

_____

_____

_____

_____

3. In Building Study Skills 6 you got some tips on how to concentrate better when you are studying. Choose a lesson from the next topic and, after previewing it, write out a plan for studying it. Include the following:

   • the total amount of time you think it should take to complete the lesson;

   • how many periods of study you will divide the work into;

   • three things that your skimming of the lesson suggests that you will learn from it.

_____

_____

_____

_____

_____

4. Assume you have been selected to do the advertising for an author slide presentation based on either "Into the Kenyan Game Reserve" or "Cajun Country." Describe four photos you would use to convey the flavor of the slide presentation. Then write a brief caption to accompany each slide that would get an audience interested in seeing the whole show. If you want, you can find actual photos and write the captions for them rather than for imaginary slides.

_____

_____

_____

_____

_____

5. Does one of the places described in this unit sound like somewhere you would like to visit? Or are you a person with no interest in traveling? If you would like to see one of these travel destinations, tell which one and why it appeals to you. If you are a person who sees no value in traveling, write to explain why you feel as you do. For either writing assignment, make your reasons as specific as you can.

_____

_____

_____

_____

_____

6. Travel programs on television are often accompanied by background music. What kind of music would you select to accompany a show based on "Moscow on the Make" or "Letter from France"? Review the selection you choose for possible musical tie-ins; then select two or three musical pieces to use with it. Write your choices, the parts of the selection they are to accompany, and your reasons for selecting them.

_____

_____

_____

_____

_____

Injustice anywhere is a threat to justice everywhere.

—Martin Luther King, Jr. (1929–1968)

DOING WHAT'S RIGHT

Red Fire Farm

Anchee Min

VOCABULARY—PART ONE

All of these words are in the selection you are about to read. Study each word and its meaning. Then answer the questions below. As you read the selection, notice how each vocabulary word is used.

remnants: small unused pieces; remains

taper: get gradually narrower at one end

leech: bloodsucking worm

plaited: braided

platoon: military unit or group

barren: unproductive; unused; desolate

hods: tray set at the end of a long handle, used for carrying bricks

muted: muffled; quiet

makeshift: temporary; created for just one occasion

mucus: slimy substance created within the nose

---

1. Which word describes a way that a person may fix his or her hair?

   _____

2. Which word could describe a stage set up for just one performance and then torn down afterwards?

   _____

3. Which word could describe land on which no crops have been planted?

   _____

4. Which word might describe the sound of a conversation that you hear through a closed door?

   _____

5. Which word might name a group on an army base?

   _____

1   I arrived at Red Fire Farm—along with many other girls in ten large trucks—late one spring afternoon in 1974. Our names had appeared on our schools' Glorious Red Lists, a great honour, but one which meant that we would have to leave home to work in another province. The farm was near the East China Sea. It consisted of endless fields of sea reeds, and rectangular grey barracks each with a long outdoor sink.

2   I was assigned to house number three, and to a small room with bunk beds for my seven room-mates. The floor was packed earth. My only private space was provided by a mosquito net that hung from thin bamboo sticks. The bed next to mine was given to a girl named Shao Ching, who, like me, was seventeen years old. Shao Ching was pale-skinned and slim as a willow. When she spoke, she looked down at the ground. Unlike the rest of us who tied our braids with standard brown rubber-bands, Shao Ching tied hers with colourful strings. She was extremely neat. No matter how tired we got after a day's heavy labour, she would walk forty-five minutes to the hot-water station and then carry back water to wash herself.

3   I was proud to be Shao Ching's friend. She showed me how she used <u>remnants</u> of fabric to make pretty underwear, finely embroidered with flowers, leaves and love-birds. She hung a string next to the little window between our beds on which she could hang her underwear to dry. In our bare room the string was like an art gallery.

4   All the girls secretly envied Shao Ching. She redesigned the clothes she was issued: her shirts to <u>taper</u> at the waist; her trousers to make her legs look longer. She was not embarrassed by her full breasts. The male soldiers stared at her whenever she passed by and when the weather got hotter, she dared to go without a bra. There was one man who was said to have burst into tears on hearing that Shao Ching was running a high fever.

5   I had become friends with Shao Ching on our first day in the rice fields. A <u>leech</u> had bitten her, and when she went to pull it out it had burrowed into her skin, leaving only a black dot on the surface. I was working alongside her; when she screamed, I called A-Lan, an experienced soldier, who showed us how we should pat the skin above the leech's head so that it would back itself out.

6   We had been greeted at the farm—as we got down from the trucks on that first afternoon—by the Company Commander, Yan. She was about twenty-three, tall, well-built, and walked with authority. She wore an old People's Liberation Army uniform, washed white and gathered at the waist with a three-inch-wide black belt. Her hair was <u>plaited</u> into two short, thick braids. She had examined us one by one, then begun to speak in a whisper, introducing herself—"My name is Yan Sheng. Yan meaning discipline; Sheng, victory"—welcoming us, and then shouting suddenly, "I have only one thing to say: Don't any of you shit on my face! Don't any of you betray the glorious name of the Advanced Seventh Company, model of the entire Red Fire Farm Army!" She'd asked if she had made her point clear.

7   Startled, we had answered, "Yes!"

8   My <u>platoon</u> leader, a bearded man called Lin, was a great admirer of Yan. During a break from work in the fields, he told us how Yan had been accepted as a member of the Party at the age of nineteen. When she had arrived five years ago, he said, the land of Red Fire Farm had been <u>barren</u>. She had led her platoon of twenty Red Guards in reclaiming it. Lin had been among them.

9   "Yan is famous for her iron shoulders," he said. "We all had blisters when we were working on irrigation channels. To remove the mud, we had to make at least twenty half-mile-trips in a day, carrying over a hundred and sixty pounds in two <u>hods</u> hanging from a shoulder-pole. Our shoulders swelled like steamed bread. Strong men like me gave up. Yan was a thin girl at that time, but she did not quit. She continued carrying the hods of mud and her blisters bled."

10   In my first days at the farm, I had seen Yan carry large loads. She had piled reed upon reed upon her head until she looked like she had a hill on her shoulders, with only her legs moving underneath.

11   Lin mentioned a fire from the last summer. "Our grain stores, straw-huts and fields of ripe crops," he said, "were destroyed. Soldiers cried. But Yan stood in front of us. One of her braids had burnt off and her clothes were smoking; she told us that our faith in Communism was all we needed to rebuild our dream. We built these houses in five months…"

12   I imagined Yan with a burnt off braid, her skin scorched by fire raging behind her. I had always admired the heroines in the revolutionary operas created by Madam Mao, Comrade Jiang Ching.

13 Without being aware of it, in a few weeks, I started to imitate Yan. My belt was only two inches wide; I wished it was an inch wider. I cut my long braids short. I tried to carry as much as I could when our platoon was sent to dig a new irrigation channel, even tried to allow my shoulder-pole to rub my bleeding blisters, though the pain was unbearable. And every night I gave speeches at meetings for confession and self-criticism.

"A good female comrade was supposed to devote all her energy, her youth, to the Revolution."

14 At one of these meetings Yan raised an important matter. It concerned Shao Ching. Two of her prettiest hand-embroidered pairs of underwear had been stolen from the line between our beds. The platoon leader suspected the male soldiers and had reported the case to the Party Committee. No one had admitted to the theft. Yan's deputy, a fierce woman named Lu, said that such behaviour shamed us all. She criticized Shao Ching for vanity and ordered her to make a confession. Yan told Shao Ching that in future she should not hang her underwear near to the window.

15 After some months on the farm, a group of us were selected for military training programmes. I was among them. We were given tuition in shooting, handling grenades, and combat. We were also called on "midnight emergency searches" when we had to pull ourselves out of the bed and be ready to leave with our rifles and flashlights in three minutes.

16 One night in early summer, the platoon leader called for me at my window and within minutes I was off with the group. There was a warm, gentle breeze. We moved briskly, almost jogging, through the reeds. When we reached the wheat fields, an order was given in a whisper: "Load!"

17 I snapped awake—this was the first order to use live ammunition—something serious had happened. I loaded my gun.

18 "Lie down!" I heard Yan's voice. "Advance!"

19 We began crawling through the wheat. It was hard to see. The male soldier in front of me stopped crawling and passed back an order, "Stand by!"

20 I lay there holding my breath, listening. The insects were singing and the wheat smelled sweet. Mosquitoes began to bite me through my clothes. There was a noise in the distance. Then silence. I thought the noise had been my imagination. After about a minute, I heard the noise again. It was two sounds. One was a man's, the other was a woman murmuring. I heard a soft, muted cry. And then my shock: I recognized the voice as Shao Ching's.

21 My only thought was: I can't let Shao Ching be caught like this. She was my best friend, the only person in my room who was open with me. She had never told me anything about being involved with a man, though I could understand why: it would be shameful to admit. A good female comrade was supposed to devote all her energy, her youth, to the Revolution; she was not permitted even to think about a man until she reached her late twenties, when marriage would be considered. I thought of the consequences Shao Ching would have to bear if she were caught. I crawled forward toward the noise. A firm hand immediately pressed me down to the ground. Yan. She seemed to know exactly what was going on.

22 As the murmuring and hard breathing became louder, I heard Yan clench her teeth together and draw in a breath, then she loosened her grip on my back and shouted suddenly, "Now!"

23 It was as if a bomb had exploded next to me. Yan turned her flashlight on Shao Ching and the man. About thirty other flashlights, including mine, were switched on at the same time.

24 Shao Ching screamed. She was in her favourite shirt—the one embroidered with pink mei flowers. The lights shone on her naked buttocks.

25 The man with Shao Ching was skinny, wore glasses and looked very bookish. He pulled up his pants and tried to run. He was caught immediately by the group led by the deputy commander, Lu,

who pulled out her rifle, and held it to the bookish man's head. He wasn't from our company, but I remembered having seen him at the market. He had smiled at Shao Ching, but when I had asked whether she knew him, she had said no.

26 Shao Ching was trembling and weeping. She scrambled back and forth for her clothes, trying to cover her buttocks with her hands.

27 I lowered my flashlight.

28 Yan slowly approached the man. "Why do you have to do this?" To my surprise, I saw that her eyes glistened with tears.

29 The man bit his lip.

30 Yan threw her belt down and ordered the male soldiers to beat the man. She walked away but stopped and said, "I'll be pleased if you can make him understand that today's woman is no longer the victim of man's desire." She took off her jacket to cover Shao Ching. "Let's go home," she said softly.

31 The bookish man didn't look guilty. As the kicking and whipping began, he struggled not to cry out.

32 I returned to the barracks with the other female soldiers. From a distance we could hear muted cries from the man and Lu shouting, "Death to the rapist!" Shao Ching could not stop whimpering.

33 A public trial was held in the dining-hall. Shao Ching had undergone four days of "intensive mind re-brushing." On a <u>makeshift</u> stage, she declared in a high, strained voice that she had been raped. The paper from which she read slipped out of her hands twice. Her bookish lover was convicted. I will never forget his expression when the death sentence was announced. As if waking from a nightmare, he looked suddenly relaxed. His bruised purple face had brightened when Shao Ching walked into the hall.

34 No one talked about the man after the execution, although he was on everyone's mind. But Shao Ching had changed. She stopped washing. Months passed. Still she hadn't washed. There were complaints about her smell. When I tried to persuade her to wash her underwear at least, she took a pair of scissors and cut it into strips. She chopped off her long braids and stopped combing her hair. <u>Mucus</u> dripped from her lips. At night, she sang songs off-key. My room-mates reported her behaviour and she was sent to the farm's hospital. The doctors referred her to a hospital in Shanghai

where she was diagnosed as having had a nervous breakdown.

35 When Shao Ching returned from the hospital six months later, I didn't recognize her. The drugs she had been prescribed had made her gain weight. She was as fat as a bear.

36 She was again given a bed in my room, where she sat quietly most of the day, staring in one direction. Her pupils sometimes moved upwards, then disappeared into her skull as if she was trying to read her own brain. Her hair was matted. I thought of the evenings when she would wash her hair after dinner, and comb and dry it as the sun set. She used to sing "My Mother Land," a song that we all knew.

> There are girls like beautiful flowers,
> Boys with strong bodies and open minds.
> To build our new China,
> We are happily working and sweating together…

Starting Time	
Finishing Time	
Reading Time	
Reading Rate	

COMPREHENSION

Read the following questions and statements. For each one, put an X in the box before the option that contains the most complete or accurate answer.

1. This selection takes place in
   ☐ a. 1994.
   ☐ b. 1984.
   ☐ c. 1974.
   ☐ d. 1964.

2. Life at Red Fire Farm was
   ☐ a. hard at the beginning but easier later.
   ☐ b. filled with groups that were jealous of each other.
   ☐ c. designed to make young people into strong individualists.
   ☐ d. regimented and difficult.

3. This writer makes her point by
   ☐ a. telling a story.
   ☐ b. presenting an argument filled with good reasons.
   ☐ c. carefully explaining what the camp looked like.
   ☐ d. letting Shao Ching tell her views about what went on.

4. A good summary of this selection would be the following statement:
   ☐ a. There is no fairness in a military camp.
   ☐ b. Women are often better soldiers than men.
   ☐ c. Vanity is a foolish shortcoming.
   ☐ d. Injustice can destroy people's lives.

5. When Shao Ching is discovered with her lover, the blame is automatically placed on
   ☐ a. her.
   ☐ b. the man.
   ☐ c. Yan.
   ☐ d. the hard conditions in the camp.

6. Shao Ching says she has been raped because
   ☐ a. it is what she now believes.
   ☐ b. she has been forced to say so.
   ☐ c. she knows her lover will betray her.
   ☐ d. this is the only way she will be allowed to go home.

7. What does the author think happens to "girls like beautiful flowers"?
   ☐ a. They get away with things others would not.
   ☐ b. They are destroyed by the system.
   ☐ c. They attract the wrong sort of men.
   ☐ d. They overcome their misfortunes and are stronger as a result.

8. When Yan speaks to Shao Ching in paragraph 30, the tone she uses is one of
   ☐ a. sorrow.
   ☐ b. anger.
   ☐ c. surprise.
   ☐ d. self-righteousness.

9. Yan was a person who
   ☐ a. had no human feelings.
   ☐ b. was jealous of Shao Ching.
   ☐ c. took her job very seriously.
   ☐ d. wanted to show that women were superior to men.

10. The statement "Our shoulders swelled like steamed bread" is a
    ☐ a. simile.
    ☐ b. metaphor.
    ☐ c. literal description.
    ☐ d. personification.

Comprehension Skills Key

1. recalling specific facts
2. retaining concepts
3. organizing facts
4. understanding the main idea
5. drawing a conclusion
6. making a judgment
7. making an inference
8. recognizing tone
9. understanding characters
10. appreciating literary forms

VOCABULARY—PART TWO

Write the word that makes the most sense in each sentence.

leech	platoon
hods	muted
mucus	

1. The sound was _____ in the barracks as the young women slept.

2. Most of them were exhausted from carrying around _____ filled with bricks.

3. There was a lot of sickness among the members of their _____ .

4. One young woman was sneezing, with _____ dripping from her nose.

5. Another had a fever and was using the old-time cure of having a _____ suck the infection from her blood.

plaited **remnants**
taper **makeshift**
barren

6. Tired of looking at their _____
   surroundings, some women did things to make
   the barracks more lively.

7. They pieced together _____ of
   cloth to create art for the walls.

8. They _____ long strands of grass
   into ropelike decorations.

9. These _____ improvements were
   only temporary, but they brightened everyone's
   spirits while they lasted

10. The women even decided to
    _____ the waists of their shirts to
    make them fit better.

Comprehension [ ]

Vocabulary [ ]

UNDERSTANDING
THROUGH WRITING

Did a girl like Shao Ching belong at a place like Red
Fire Farm? Think about the purpose of the place and
the way of life there before you answer. Then write
your opinion. Use details from the story to support
what you say.

_____

_____

_____

_____

_____

_____

_____

BUILDING STUDY SKILLS

Read the following passage and answer the questions that follow it.

Terminal Signals

We have been looking at Forward Signals and Summary Signals, two types of signals that urge the reader
on, words that indicate the continuance of the same
thoughts and ideas.

Yet another type of signal exists. The Terminal Signal plays a critical role in any written matter.

As the label suggests, Terminal Signals tell the
reader that the author is concluding his or her remarks.
They announce that the author has developed all the
thoughts to be presented and that he or she is about to
sum them up or draw a conclusion. Some Terminal
Signals are *as a result, to summarize, finally,* and *in
conclusion.* They tell the reader that an ongoing
thought is about to be terminated.

The main difference between Summary and Terminal Signals is that sense of finality. Summary Signals
indicate a pause in the forward motion of a thought.
The writer uses the pause not only to sum up the original ideas, but also to extend the subject further. He or
she is not yet ready to state a final conclusion.

Terminal Signals, on the other hand, end the account
in an obvious way. Observe the following use of a Terminal Signal: "Once the police patrols had been doubled, the cat burglar was caught. *As a result,* this
burglar's days of catting are all over." The phrase *as a
result* makes it plain that the author has said everything
she intends to say on the subject.

1. The last Forward Signals to be considered are the
   _____ Signals.

2. As the name suggests, these signals announce the
   _____ of the presentation.

3. The ideas following these last statements will summarize or draw a _____ .

4. Terminal Signals indicate a sense of
   _____ .

5. In a paper on "Red Fire Farm," a Terminal Signal
   like *in conclusion* makes it plain that the writer has
   said all he _____ to say.

The Cow-Tail Switch

West African Folktale

READING PURPOSE—
In this selection, a ruler decides which of his sons to reward. As you read, try to decide whom he will choose and if his decision is fair.

VOCABULARY—PART ONE

All of these words are in the selection you are about to read. Study each word and its meaning. Then answer the questions below. As you read the selection, notice how each vocabulary word is used.

cassava: tropical plant that tapioca is made from

grazed: fed on grass and foliage

seeped: leaked slowly

hover: hang suspended; linger

mortars: bowls or other containers for pounding

detained: delayed

sinews: bands of tough tissue connecting muscles to bones; tendons

cowry: highly polished, brightly colored shell of a sea creature

switch: tuft of hair from the end of a tail

clamor: loud outcry

1. Which word could be used in talking about how water gradually came through a crack in a wall?

_____

2. Which word names a plant used for food?

_____

3. Which word could describe the noise of a crowd as they demand that a concert begin?

_____

4. Which word describes how cattle fed themselves?

_____

5. Which word names parts of a human body?

_____

1   Near the edge of the Liberian rain forest, on a hill overlooking the Cavally River, was the village of Kundi. Its rice and cassava fields spread in all directions. Cattle grazed in the grassland near the river. Smoke from the fires in the round clay houses seeped through the palmleaf roofs, and from a distance these faint columns of smoke seemed to hover over the village. Men and boys fished in the river with nets, and women pounded grain in wooden mortars before the houses.

2   In this village, with his wife and many children, lived a hunter by the name of Ogaloussa.

3   One morning Ogaloussa took his weapons down from the wall of his house and went into the forest to hunt. His wife and his children went to tend their fields, and drove their cattle out to graze. The day passed, and they ate their evening meal of manioc and fish. Darkness came, but Ogaloussa didn't return.

4   Another day went by, and still Ogaloussa didn't come back. They talked about it and wondered what could have detained him. A week passed, then a month. Sometimes Ogaloussa's sons mentioned that he hadn't come home. The family cared for the crops, and the sons hunted for game, but after a while they no longer talked about Ogaloussa's disappearance.

5   Then, one day, another son was born to Ogaloussa's wife. His name was Puli. Puli grew older. He began to sit up and crawl. The time came when Puli began to talk, and the first thing he said was, "Where is my father?"

6   The other sons looked across the ricefields.

7   "Yes," one of them said. "Where is Father?"

8   "He should have returned long ago," another one said.

9   "Something must have happened. We ought to look for him," a third son said.

10   "He went into the forest, but where will we find him?" another one asked.

11   "I saw him go," one of them said. "He went that way, across the river. Let us follow the trail and search for him."

12   So the sons took their weapons and started out to look for Ogaloussa. When they were deep among the great trees and vines of the forest they lost the trail. They searched in the forest until one of them found the trail again. They followed it until they lost the way once more, and then another son found the trail. It was dark in the forest, and many times they became lost. Each time another son found the way. At last they came to a clearing among the trees, and there on the ground scattered about lay Ogaloussa's bones and his rusted weapons. They knew then that Ogaloussa had been killed in the hunt.

13   One of the sons stepped forward and said, "I know how to put a dead person's bones together." He gathered all of Ogaloussa's bones and put them together, each in its right place.

14   Another son said, "I have knowledge too. I know how to cover the skeleton with sinews and flesh." He went to work, and covered Ogaloussa's bones with sinews and flesh.

15   A third son said, "I have the power to put blood into a body." He went forward and put blood into Ogaloussa's veins, and then he stepped aside.

16   Another of the sons said, "I can put breath into a body." He did his work, and when he was through they saw Ogaloussa's chest rise and fall.

17   "I can give the power of movement to a body," another of them said. He put the power of movement into his father's body, and Ogaloussa sat up and opened his eyes.

18   "I can give him the power of speech," another son said. He gave the body the power of speech, and then he stepped back.

19   Ogaloussa looked around him. He stood up.

20   "Where are my weapons?" he asked.

21   They picked up his rusted weapons from the grass where they lay and gave them to him. They then returned the way they had come, through the forest and the ricefields, until they had arrived once more in the village.

22   Ogaloussa went into his house. His wife prepared a bath for him and he bathed. She prepared food for him and he ate. Four days he remained in the house, and on the fifth day he came out and shaved his head, because this was what people did when they came back from the land of the dead.

23   Afterwards he killed a cow for a great feast. He took the cow's tail and braided it. He decorated it with beads and cowry shells and bits of shiny metal. It was a beautiful thing. Ogaloussa carried it with him to important affairs. When there was a dance or an important ceremony he always had it with him. The people of the village thought it was the most beautiful cow-tail switch they had ever seen.

24   Soon there was a celebration in the village because Ogaloussa had returned from the dead. The people dressed in their best clothes, the

musicians brought out their instruments, and a big dance began. The drummers beat their drums and the women sang. The people drank much palm wine. Everyone was happy.

25 Ogaloussa carried his cow-tail <u>switch</u>, and everyone admired it. Some of the men grew bold and came forward to Ogaloussa and asked for the cow-tail switch, but Ogaloussa kept it in his hand. Now and then there was a <u>clamor</u> and much confusion as many people asked for it at once. The women and children begged for it too, but Ogaloussa refused them all.

26 Finally he stood up to talk. The dancing stopped and people came close to hear what Ogaloussa had to say.

27 "A long time ago I went into the forest," Ogaloussa said. "While I was hunting I was killed by a leopard. Then my sons came for me. They brought me back from the land of the dead to my village. I will give this cow-tail switch to one of my sons. All of them have done something to bring me back from the dead, but I have only one cow tail to give. I shall give it to the one who did the most to bring me home."

28 So an argument started.

29 "He will give it to me!" one of the sons said. "It was I who did the most, for I found the trail in the forest when it was lost."

30 "No, he will give it to me!" another son said. "It was I who put his bones together!"

31 "It was I who covered his bones with sinews and flesh!" another said. "He will give it to me!"

32 "It was I who gave him the power of movement!" another son said. "I deserve it most!"

33 Another son said it was he who should have the switch, because he had put blood in Ogaloussa's veins. Another claimed it because he had put breath in the body. Each of the sons argued his right to possess the wonderful cow-tail switch.

34 Before long not only the sons but the other people of the village were talking. Some of them argued that the son who had put blood in

"I shall give it to the one who did the most to bring me home."

Ogaloussa's veins should get the switch, others that the one who had given Ogaloussa's breath should get it. Some of them believed that all of the sons had done equal things, and that they should share it. They argued back and forth this way until Ogaloussa asked them to be quiet.

35 "To this son I will give the cow-tail switch, for I owe most to him," Ogaloussa said.

36 He came forward and bent low and handed it to Puli, the little boy who had been born while Ogaloussa was in the forest.

37 The people of the village remembered then that the child's first words had been, "Where is my father?" They knew that Ogaloussa was right.

38 For it was a saying among them that a man is not really dead until he is forgotten.

Starting Time	
Finishing Time	
Reading Time	
Reading Rate	

COMPREHENSION

Read the following questions and statements. For each one, put an X in the box before the option that contains the most complete or accurate answer.

1. Ogaloussa's decision to give the cow's tail to his youngest son was
   ☐ a. supported strongly by the villagers.
   ☐ b. strongly debated.
   ☐ c. resented by his sons.
   ☐ d. misunderstood by Puli.

2. According to the customs of Kundi, the worst thing people could do to a dead man was to
 ☐ a. bury him.
 ☐ b. forget him.
 ☐ c. honor him.
 ☐ d. scorn him.

3. The details in paragraph 12 are presented
 ☐ a. from least to most important.
 ☐ b. in spatial order.
 ☐ c. in time order.
 ☐ d. by giving specific evidence to back up a topic sentence.

4. The purpose of the selection is to
 ☐ a. embarrass a forgetful wife.
 ☐ b. start a family argument.
 ☐ c. teach a lesson.
 ☐ d. describe African customs.

5. A person who returned from the land of the dead was expected to
 ☐ a. make a cow-tail switch.
 ☐ b. honor his sons.
 ☐ c. shave his head.
 ☐ d. speak a new language.

6. The people of Kundi considered it a great honor to be
 ☐ a. invited to a great feast.
 ☐ b. recalled from the land of the dead.
 ☐ c. asked to sing and dance.
 ☐ d. awarded a braided cow's tail.

7. In the society of Kundi,
 ☐ a. a father's word was law.
 ☐ b. everyone had a say in important decisions.
 ☐ c. a mother and father consulted together before reaching a decision.
 ☐ d. the youngest child was always favored.

8. The atmosphere at the beginning of the selection is
 ☐ a. strained and worried.
 ☐ b. orderly and peaceful.
 ☐ c. noisy and troubled.
 ☐ d. dark and suspicious.

9. Ogaloussa's older sons were
 ☐ a. heartless.   ☐ c. evil.
 ☐ b. forgetful.   ☐ d. jealous.

10. The selection contains elements that involve
 ☐ a. humor.
 ☐ b. biography.
 ☐ c. talking animals.
 ☐ d. the supernatural.

Comprehension Skills Key

1. recalling specific facts
2. retaining concepts
3. organizing facts
4. understanding the main idea
5. drawing a conclusion
6. making a judgment
7. making an inference
8. recognizing tone
9. understanding characters
10. appreciating literary forms

VOCABULARY—PART TWO

Write the word that makes the most sense in each sentence.

cassava   sinews
grazed   mortars
switch

1. The women from the village pounded grain in their _____ .

2. With this grain and the _____ that grew nearby, they would create a typical evening meal.

3. On special occasions they would butcher one of the cows that _____ in the nearby field.

4. The cow's _____ would be separated from its bones and used as a kind of rope.

5. The _____ , which came from the tail, would be decorated and saved for special occasions.

detained   seeped
hover   clamor
cowry

6. A young man from the village had been

    _____ so long on a hunting trip

    that everyone feared he was dead.

7. His friends went to search for him, each wearing

    a _____ shell for good luck.

8. The silence of the forest was broken by a

    _____ as they found their

    friend's body.

9. His skull was cracked open, and his blood

    _____ onto the ground.

10. He was dead, but his friends could see his spirit

    _____ just above his body.

Comprehension [ ]

Vocabulary [ ]

UNDERSTANDING THROUGH WRITING

How do you think the other sons will react to the father's decision? Write a paragraph or two stating your opinion and telling why you think as you do.

_____

_____

_____

_____

_____

_____

_____

_____

_____

BUILDING STUDY SKILLS

Read the following passage and answer the questions that follow it.

Counter Signals

We have been looking at Forward Signals, which tell the reader that a thought is continuing, that more of the same is coming. We have also discussed Terminal Signals, which the writer uses to tell the reader that an ongoing thought is about to come to an end.

The last signal we will examine does a different job; it signals a reversal of the thought. Called a Counter Signal, this device turns the thought sharply in a different direction. It tells the reader to be alert, because a countering idea is soon to appear.

Some common Counter Signals are *but, yet, nevertheless, otherwise, although, despite, in spite of, no, not, on the contrary,* and *however.* They are all used to introduce an idea that not only differs from what has gone before but also leads the reader in a new direction.

By far the most common Counter Signal is *but.* It is a little word, but it's packed with meaning. Check to see how it affects the sense of the passage.

Indeed, when you come upon any of the Counter Signals, realize that the thought is not going forward any longer, that it has stopped. And in textbooks especially, be alert for Counter Signals. They indicate that the author has come to a turn in the road and is about to go in a different direction.

1. The final signals to be considered are called

    _____ .

2. These signals turn the thought in a sharply

    different _____ .

3. *But* is the most powerful word, because it can af-

    fect the entire _____ of the passage.

4. In the sentence "After a while they no longer

    talked about Ogaloussa's disappearance," the

    Counter Signal is _____ .

5. In the sentence "Some of the men grew bold and

    asked for the cow-tail switch, but Ogaloussa kept it

    in his hand," the word *but* signals a

    _____ of the thought.

13

Then Came the Famous
Kristallnacht

Elise Radell (as told to Joan Morrison and Charlotte Fox Zabusky)

READING PURPOSE—
In this selection, the writer tells how her family responded when the Nazis began persecuting Jews in Germany just before World War II began. Read to see if you share her feelings about their reactions

VOCABULARY—PART ONE

All of these words are in the selection you are about to read. Study each word and its meaning. Then answer the questions below. As you read the selection, notice how each vocabulary word is used.

integrated: blended or mixed together
breakfront: large cabinet for storing china
stunned: shocked; astonished
eventually: in due time

quota: a set number or amount
nationalist: person with strong patriotic feelings about his/her country
atheist: person who does not believe in God
deported: sent out of a country against one's will
brooch: ornamental pin usually worn at the neckline of a dress
milieu: surroundings; environment

---

1. Which word names a piece of furniture?

_____

2. Which word names something you could purchase in a jewelry store?

_____

3. Which word describes a gathering in which people of all races are mixed together?

_____

4. Which word describes how you might feel if you heard your best friend was in a serious car accident?

_____

5. Which word names a person whom you might expect to lead in the singing of "The Star Spangled Banner"?

_____

1   I was born in 1931 and Hitler came to power in 1933. As a little girl I never noticed anything. We were much integrated into the society. We had friends that were Jewish, that were non-Jewish. There never seemed to be any difference. But by 1937 or 1938, the Brown Shirts came along. All of a sudden, we became very much aware that we were Jews. We didn't know quite what to do with it. I remember going to school one day and somebody said to me, "You're Jewish," and threw a rock at me. I came home and I said to my mom and dad, "What is this being Jewish? Other people are Catholic. There are a lot of Lutherans and there are all kinds of churches, and why are they throwing stones at me?" And my parents said, "Well, that's the way it is." And then they took me out of regular public school and they took a private tutor for me—a young man who used to come to our house every day. I remember sitting in the dining room with him and we studied. I didn't study very well because I liked him more as a friend than as a teacher. I was about seven or eight then.

2   My grandfather owned a very large apartment house, where we lived. In fact, it was the first apartment house in Ludwigshafen, where I was born, that had glass doors that opened and an elevator. It was on the main street, and I remember the Nazis, on the days when there were parades for the Nazis, coming onto our dining room balcony; because our dining room balcony faced the main street in Ludwigshafen and it had to have a flagpole holder. And they came in every time there was a parade and put up the swastika flag. I didn't like that. I didn't like them and I didn't like that.

3   Then came the famous *Kristallnacht*.[1] I don't remember the exact date. That morning, Mina, the maid, and I were going to get milk from the milk store. As we opened the door, the SS[2] was there. They pushed us aside and came into the house. "*Guten Morgen*,"[3] they said, "*Guten Morgen*," I remember. They were very polite and then they went about this utter destruction with axes. They knew exactly how to do it. We had a breakfront in the dining room and it was one piece of teakwood, maybe seven feet long, and they knew just how to

wreck it with one ax. Zzaszhh! Just ruined the whole thing. And the china closet was knocked all over and the pictures on the wall, with just one rip in each, and the furniture all just went. They were scientific about it. They had been told exactly how to go about it with the least amount of work. The pillows were ripped and the feathers—at that time there were feathers, you know—they just flew all over the house, and it was total destruction. Just ruined everything. My grandmother locked herself in the bathroom. The rest of us just stood and watched this destruction. Everyone was in shock. There was no fighting back. We were just stunned. Afterward, they took all the Jewish men, put them in jail, and then transported them to Dachau.[4]

4   My father had been out of town on business and didn't come home until the next day. And then, out of some strange, unbelievable loyalty or honor or whatever the Germans were brought up to believe, when he came home and saw that all the Jewish men were gone, he went to the police station and gave himself up.

5   Now, I, as a Jew, can't quite understand how the German Jews did this; how my father could come back and turn himself in. But, being raised his whole life as an honorable citizen, to him this was the height of being honorable. And it's very hard for me to accept. I can understand intellectually; I don't understand it emotionally....

6   After this, all the German Jewish women and children began to live together. I remember a cousin, a neighbor, another neighbor; we all lived in our apartment. We had the largest apartment. The train from Dachau to Ludwigshafen came at 2:10 every morning, and everybody woke up at 2:10 A.M., because you never knew who would come home. We had a distant aunt and her daughter living with us, and one night her husband came home and it was my Uncle Julius. I loved him dearly before that. And he walked into our house and I wouldn't look at him and I said, "How come you didn't bring my daddy?" I just couldn't understand how he came home without my daddy.

7   Later, much later, eventually my daddy came home. My father was six-foot-one then, and tall and handsome, as a daughter sees her daddy—an eight-year-old daughter. And he had all his hair shaved off and he was down to ninety pounds. He

---

[1]*Kristallnacht:* "crystal night," referring to the broken glass left after a night in November 1938 when organized mobs of Nazis looted, pillaged, and burned Jewish shops, synagogues, and homes
[2]*SS:* abbreviation of *Schutzstaffel* ("elite guard"), a unit of Nazis whose duties included policing and exterminating people deemed undesirable
[3]*Guten Morgen:* "Good morning"

[4]*Dachau:* a city in southwestern Germany that became the site of a concentration camp during Nazi rule

came home and he never spoke about it again. Never mentioned it. It must have been so unbelievably terrible. But he came home. All I remember is his shaven head and that he was very skinny. But he hugged me and kissed me and he said hello. "*Guten Tag*,[5] Lisel. Everything's all right."

"[We] just stood and watched this destruction. Everyone was in shock. There was no fighting back."

8   Those who could got boat tickets then to America, to Shanghai, wherever they could go. You couldn't get a visa to America unless you had relatives there. I think Roosevelt could have tried to open the quota a little bit. Maybe he did try; I don't know. But we had an aunt who had come to the U.S. in 1936, and she did everything she could for us. We had to go to Stuttgart, which was the center where all the visas and passports were given. My mother always took me along because I didn't look Jewish. I had blue eyes and blond hair at the time. We had to go by train, I remember. We finally managed to get the visas and everything, and we got on a boat and landed here in August 1939. The last trip over.

9   We begged my grandparents to come with us, but my grandfather was a great German nationalist. Not a religious man. He just didn't believe in God, and, therefore, what sense did temple make or religion make? He was an atheist. He was a German. And he said, "No. Nothing will happen to me." He wouldn't go. But now I think back—I have a feeling my grandfather knew my grandmother wouldn't make it through the physical. She was a very sick woman then. So he stayed with her. First they were deported to France, and then they were on one of those trains. The last we ever heard. In fact, we have a picture of them going on one of those trains—stepping up to the car that was going to go to Poland or wherever they went to be gassed. A friend of a friend saw them and took a picture. I have the picture now. I never look at it....

Right to the bitter end they were properly dressed. My grandfather had on a tie and a white shirt, and my grandmother had a dress on and a brooch and whatever shoes she had. And they got into that train! That's what I say about the German Jews. Down to the bitter end they had a false dignity. That's what they knew and that's what they were told to do, and they did it in the most elegant and dignified way they knew how. Right down to the gas chamber. And I'm sure that they walked into that gas chamber with their heads held high and that was it.... [Breaks down.]

10   I say, "Why didn't they fight? Why didn't we all fight back?" But if you're raised in a certain milieu, you cannot change. And besides, the fight would have been hopeless. That's something we know. The Poles' fight was hopeless, too, but at least they did it. You know, I'm torn. I always knew, after I got my senses back and was settled, I said, "I never could marry a German Jew," because I don't quite believe in going into the death chamber with your head held high, without somehow, somewhere, fighting back. It might be a terrible thing for me to say. In a way, I feel like a traitor when I think that, and, in another way, I feel, "Well, I'm an individual. I'm a free soul. I can begin to believe the way I would believe—and choose what I would choose." I don't blame my parents, because there were too many who did it the same way. But I don't think I could do it....

Starting Time	
Finishing Time	
Reading Time	
Reading Rate	

---

[5]*Guten Tag:* "Good day"

COMPREHENSION

Read the following questions and statements. For each one, put an X in the box before the option that contains the most complete or accurate answer.

1. Elise Radell now lives in
   - ☐ a. Germany.
   - ☐ b. Canada.
   - ☐ c. the United States.
   - ☐ d. France.

2. Radell has a lot of trouble accepting
   - ☐ a. her non-Jewish relatives on her husband's side of the family.
   - ☐ b. how passive and obedient her family were.
   - ☐ c. the number of people the Nazis killed.
   - ☐ d. that her children are not interested in her story.

3. The story begins
   - ☐ a. when Radell is a young schoolgirl.
   - ☐ b. when Radell gets married.
   - ☐ c. on Kristallnacht.
   - ☐ d. when Radell's father turns himself in.

4. A title for this selection that sums up its main idea might be
   - ☐ a. Honor—or Survival?
   - ☐ b. Leaving Germany.
   - ☐ c. Children, Parents, and Grandparents.
   - ☐ d. Fighting the Nazis.

5. Before the Nazis took over, Radell's family was
   - ☐ a. very poor.
   - ☐ b. struggling to get by.
   - ☐ c. pretty well off.
   - ☐ d. the richest family in their town.

6. Because he was a nationalist, Radell's grandfather believed that
   - ☐ a. German money could buy his way out of anything.
   - ☐ b. the younger family members were smart to leave.
   - ☐ c. after the war Germany would rise again.
   - ☐ d. his country would never do anything bad.

7. Radell is probably married to
   - ☐ a. a German Jew.
   - ☐ b. a Jew, but not a German Jew.
   - ☐ c. a Christian.
   - ☐ d. an Arab.

8. In describing most of the things her family did, Radell's tone is one of
   - ☐ a. intense anger.
   - ☐ b. total unconcern.
   - ☐ c. deep sympathy.
   - ☐ d. uncomprehending astonishment.

9. Radell comes across as a woman
   - ☐ a. unwilling to sit back and tolerate injustice.
   - ☐ b. grateful to her country for the freedom it offers her.
   - ☐ c. resentful of her older relatives.
   - ☐ d. who will never find happiness.

10. This story is told by a
   - ☐ a. third-person limited narrator.
   - ☐ b. third-person omniscient narrator.
   - ☐ c. second-person narrator.
   - ☐ d. first-person narrator.

Comprehension Skills Key

1. recalling specific facts
2. retaining concepts
3. organizing facts
4. understanding the main idea
5. drawing a conclusion
6. making a judgment
7. making an inference
8. recognizing tone
9. understanding characters
10. appreciating literary forms

VOCABULARY—PART TWO

Write the word that makes the most sense in each sentence.

integrated	**stunned**
eventually	**deported**
milieu	

1. The surprise attacks on *Kristallnacht* left many Jews _____ and disbelieving.

2. They had feared that the Nazis would come after them _____ , but not so quickly and suddenly.

3. Because they had been so well _____ into German society, they were very surprised to be singled out now.

4. A few, believing they could start over in another country, asked to be _____ .

5. Living in a new _____ might help them forget about their native land.

quota	**nationalist**
atheist	**breakfront**
brooch	

6. If a woman was a(n) _____ , she might refuse to believe that her country would not love her in return.

7. She might believe instead that the country had set a _____ and that only a few people would be harmed.

8. Such a woman might hide her valuables behind the china in her _____ .

9. She might give her favorite _____ and other jewelry to a neighbor for safekeeping.

10. Only a(n) _____ would not believe in a God that would protect people.

Comprehension [   ]

Vocabulary [   ]

UNDERSTANDING THROUGH WRITING

Is Radell right in reacting as she does to the way her father and grandfather dealt with the Nazis? Should they have fought harder to protect themselves? Write your opinions on this subject. Be sure to explain why you feel as you do.

_____

_____

_____

_____

_____

_____

_____

_____

_____

_____

_____

BUILDING STUDY SKILLS

Read the following passage and answer the questions that follow it.

Mastering the Text, I

According to the old saying, laborers are only as good as their tools. That is only true, of course, if the laborers know how to use the tools. For students, one tool of learning is textbooks, and the quality of students' work depends largely on how well they use those books.

Fortunately, most modern textbooks are well organized. Publishers try to be sure that their texts are up-to-date, broad in scope, and direct. And students can take advantage of those very features. One place to begin is by considering the authors.

Evaluate the Authors. Naturally, authors know more about the subject than you do; you cannot judge them on that basis. But you can try to learn about their background and experience. Are they professors? If so, where do they teach? In addition to teaching, do they work in the field? That information may tell you whether their approach is practical—based on the real world—or only theoretical. The level at which someone teaches may tell you how general or detailed that author's writing will be.

In looking for such background information, it is helpful to read authors' prefaces or introductions. There you will learn if they regard the text as an intensive discussion or a broad survey. You may also find out if they plan to draw on their experiences in the field. Most importantly, you will be able to examine an author's reason for writing the book. You will learn what is expected of you and why the author considers the subject useful and necessary. Any ideas for you to keep in mind as you use the text should be covered in the preface. Such introductory remarks are designed to get you off to a good start.

In addition, you should check the copyright date to make sure that the book is current. In today's world, new information accumulates hourly. Therefore it is essential that textbook material is timely enough to be of use.

1. It is a good idea for a student to

   _____ about the author's background and experience.

2. Working in the field gives the author a

   _____ approach to the subject.

3. An individual like Elise Radell knows what she is talking about because she is speaking from first-hand _____ .

4. The first opportunity for the author to address the reader is offered by the _____ .

5. When using a textbook, it is important to check the _____ date to see if the author's ideas are current.

14

Children of the A-Bomb

Atsuko Tsujioka (as told to Dr. Arata Osada)

READING PURPOSE—
This selection is a firsthand account of what it was like to be in Hiroshima, Japan, when American planes dropped the atomic bomb there in an effort to end World War II. As you read, decide whether you think this bombing could be justified.

VOCABULARY—PART ONE

All of these words are in the selection you are about to read. Study each word and its meaning. Then answer the questions below. As you read the selection, notice how each vocabulary word is used.

abruptly: suddenly

cistern: tank below ground for storing water

imploringly: in a begging or entreating manner

mingled: combined; blended

obsessed: intensely concerned with

pitiable: arousing or deserving pity

pessimistic: having a tendency to look at the bad side of things

stimulates: encourages; rouses to action

beneficial: helpful; bringing about good

annihilate: totally destroy

---

1. Which word describes a person who expects that bad things are going to happen?

2. Which word describes a mother who is so worried about her baby that she checks on it every ten minutes all night?

3. Which word describes what two groups of friends did who met and mixed together at a party?

4. Which word might describe what a roaring fire that burns down an entire city block has done?

5. Which word might you use in describing someone you felt sorry for?

1   Ah, that instant! I felt as though I had been struck on the back with something like a big hammer, and thrown into boiling oil. For some time I was unconscious. When I abruptly came to again, everything around me was smothered in black smoke; it was all like a dream or something that didn't make sense. My chest hurt, I could barely breathe, and I thought "This is the end!" I pressed my chest tightly and lay face down on the ground, and ever so many times I called for help:

2   "Mother!" "Mother!" "Father!" but of course in that place there was no answer from Mother, no answer from Father.

3   …I recovered my senses. Through a darkness like the bottom of Hell I could hear the voices of the other students calling for their mothers. I could barely sense the fact that the students seemed to be running away from that place. I immediately got up, and without any definite idea of escaping I just frantically ran in the direction they were all taking. As we came close to Tsurumi Bridge a red hot electric wire wrapped itself around both my ankles. I don't know how I managed to pull it off, and as though I were moving in a dream I reached the end of the bridge. By this time everything had long since changed to white smoke. The place where I had been working was Tanaka-cho, a little more than 600 yards from the center of the explosion. Although I should have been at a place straight in from Tsurumi Bridge, I seemed to have been blown a good way to the north, and I felt as though the directions were all changed around.

4   At the base of the bridge, inside a big cistern that had been dug out there, was a mother weeping and holding above her head a naked baby that was burned bright red all over its body, and another mother was crying and sobbing as she gave her burned breast to her baby. In the cistern the students stood with only their heads above the water and their two hands, which they clasped as they imploringly cried and screamed, calling for their parents. But every single person who passed was wounded, all of them, and there was no one to turn to for help. The singed hair on people's heads was frizzled up and whitish, and covered with dust—from their appearance you couldn't believe that they were human creatures of this world. Looking at these people made me think suddenly "It can't be possible that I—." I looked at my two hands and found them covered with blood, and from my arms something that looked like rags was hanging

and inside I could see the healthy-looking flesh with its mingled colors of white, red, and black…. I could feel my face gradually swelling up, but there was nothing I could do about it, and when some of my friends suggested that we try to return to our homes in the suburbs, I set out with them. As we walked along, fires were blazing high on both sides of us, and my back was painfully hot. From inside the wreckage of the houses we would hear screaming voices calling "Help!" and then the flames would swallow up everything. A child of about six, all covered with blood, holding a kitchen pot in his arms, was facing a burning house, stamping his feet and screaming something. I was in such a state that I didn't even know what to do about myself, so I could hardly attempt to be much help to him, and there was nothing to do but let him go. I wonder what happened to those people? Those people trapped under the houses? The four of us, simply obsessed with the idea of reaching home at the earliest possible minute, hurried along in just the opposite direction from that of the fleeing townspeople—straight toward the center of the blast area. However when we came to Inarimachi, we found that the iron bridge had collapsed and we could not go any farther. We turned about there and ran toward Futaba Hill. When we were close to the foot of the hill I simply couldn't make my legs carry me another step.

5   "Wait for me. Please wait for me," I said, and practically crawling, I finally reached the foot of the hill. Luckily there were some kind soldiers from a medical unit there, and they carried me up the hill to a place where I could lie down. There they gave first aid treatment right away. It seemed that I had received a terrific blow on the back of my head, and there were fragments of roof tile left there. They pulled these out and bandaged the wound for me.

6   "You just lie there quietly. Your teacher will surely be along any minute now to take care of you," they said to comfort me.

7   But no matter how long I waited, my teacher didn't come. (Our teachers themselves were severely wounded; some of them died on the afternoon of the sixth, and all of them were dead by the next day.)

8   Finally the soldiers couldn't wait any longer, and they carried us one by one on their backs down to the barracks at the foot of the hill. A Red Cross flag was waving there. They carried us inside and

asked the doctors to take care of us right away. But there were so many wounded people that we had to wait a very long time for our turn to come. In the meantime my strength was exhausted and I couldn't even keep myself standing up. At last they gave us treatment, and we spent the night there. The big buildings in the city were burning steadily, bright red against the dark sky. As the night wore on, the barracks gradually filled to overflowing with moaning voices—over in one corner someone shrieking "Bring me a straw mat if there's nothing better," and here a patient rolling about even on top of people too badly burned to move.

9   The first night came to an end. From earliest morning voices calling "Water, water" came from every side. I too was so thirsty I could hardly bear it. Inside the barracks there was a sink with water in it. Even though I knew that all sorts of things drained into it and the water was dirty, I scooped up some of that milk-coffee-colored water with my shoe and drank it. Maybe it is because I was normally healthy—anyway my mind was perfectly clear even though I had that severe wound, and since I knew there was a stream running right behind the barracks, I got up and took that shoe and went and drank and drank. And after that any number of times I brought water and gave it to the people who were lying near me and to the soldiers who were wounded....

10   My friends, and the other people too, could not move after they once lay down. Their backs and arms and legs were all slippery where the skin had peeled off, and even if I wanted to raise them up, there was no place I could take hold of them. From about noon of the second day people began to come in a few at a time. I got a white rice-ball from those people, but since my whole face was burned and I couldn't open my mouth very well, I spilled the grains of rice all around when I tried to eat, and only a little bit of it finally ended up in my

"Can it really be said that a thing which takes several hundred thousand lives at one time is true scientific development?"

mouth. By the third day I too was all swollen up, even around my eyes, and I had to lie there beside my friends unable to move at all....

11   My father and four or five of our neighbors were searching around for me day after day and finally on the evening of the third day they discovered me in one corner of the barracks at the foot of Futaba Hill. On my blouse there was sewn a name-tag that my father had written for me; the letters had been burned out just as though that part of the cloth had been eaten away by moths, and it was by this that they were able to find me.

12   "Atchan. This is Father."

13   When he said that, I was so happy that I couldn't say a word—I could only nod my head. My swollen eyes wouldn't open, so I couldn't see my father's face. This is how I was rescued.

14   Even now the scars of those wounds remain over my whole body. On my head, my face, my arms, my legs and my chest. As I stroke these blackish-red raised scars on my arms, and every time I look in a mirror at this face of mine which is not like my face, and think that never again will I be able to see my former face and that I have to live my life forever in this condition, it becomes too sad to bear. At the time I lost hope for the future. And not for a single moment could I get rid of the feeling that I had become a cripple. And naturally, for that reason I hated to meet people. And along with that, I couldn't get out of my mind the thought that so many of my good friends, and the teachers who had taken care of me so lovingly, had died under such pitiable circumstances, and I was continually choked with tears. No matter what I thought about, I was likely to be suspicious, and I took a pessimistic attitude toward everything. And my voice, which until now had been a pleasant one that all my friends liked, was lost all at once and became a hoarse voice without any volume. Every time I think about these things, my chest feels as though a terribly tight band is closing around it.

15 But with human beings, it isn't only a beautiful outward appearance that is good. True beauty, worthy of a human being, takes away an ugly appearance and makes it into a splendid one. When I first realized that, my spirit softened somewhat. At the present time, with a fresh hope for life, and studying earnestly to discipline both my body and spirit, I cannot help seeking the inner sort of beauty which comes from a cultivated mind.

16 Science—what in the world is this science? Can it really be said that a thing which takes several hundred thousand human lives at one time is true scientific development? No, science ought to be something that to the very last <u>stimulates</u> those advancements of civilization which are <u>beneficial</u> to mankind. Moreover, the mission of science is to raise the standard of living of mankind. It ought never to be such a thing as would <u>annihilate</u> the life of mankind. It is also obvious that the power of the atom, instead of being thus used as a means of making human beings lose their lives, ought to be turned to the advancement of human civilization. It is my hope that in the future such a tragic event as this will never make a second appearance in this world. And I want things to work out so that atomic energy will be the power which will give birth to a peaceful world. I believe there is no necessity for mankind to experience directly such suffering.

Starting Time ___

Finishing Time ___

Reading Time ___

Reading Rate ___

COMPREHENSION

Read the following questions and statements. For each one, put an X in the box before the option that contains the most complete or accurate answer.

1. When the blast came, the author was
   - ☐ a. working at Tanaka-cho.
   - ☐ b. asleep at her parents' house.
   - ☐ c. in a cistern.
   - ☐ d. at her friend's house.

2. The narrator realized that she was badly injured after she
   - ☐ a. could not keep up with her friends.
   - ☐ b. compared herself to the other victims.
   - ☐ c. could not satisfy her thirst.
   - ☐ d. tried to help the trapped victims.

3. After the blast, the narrator first tried to get to
   - ☐ a. Futaba Hill.
   - ☐ b. Tsurumi Bridge.
   - ☐ c. her parents' home.
   - ☐ d. her school.

4. Which of the following statements best expresses the main idea of the selection?
   - ☐ a. The power of the atom is a regrettable scientific discovery.
   - ☐ b. People can never expect to benefit from the use of atomic power.
   - ☐ c. Science should never be used to do harm to people.
   - ☐ d. Intellectual accomplishments are superior to physical accomplishments.

5. An atomic blast causes not only destruction, suffering, and death but also
   - ☐ a. makes rescue almost impossible.
   - ☐ b. causes people to become selfish.
   - ☐ c. transforms victims into volunteers.
   - ☐ d. reduces everything to rubble.

6. Those who could walk were unable to help the trapped victims. This must have been
   - ☐ a. held against them.
   - ☐ b. cruel and selfish.
   - ☐ c. difficult to bear.
   - ☐ d. merciful and humane.

7. The victims of atomic radiation all seem to
   - ☐ a. require sleep.
   - ☐ b. walk slowly.
   - ☐ c. crave water.
   - ☐ d. fear noise.

8. The atmosphere at the beginning of the selection is one of
   - ☐ a. disgust and revulsion.
   - ☐ b. shock and helplessness.
   - ☐ c. shame and sorrow.
   - ☐ d. suffering and indifference.

9. At the barracks, the narrator wanted to
   - ☐ a. help fellow victims.
   - ☐ b. die.
   - ☐ c. seek revenge.
   - ☐ d. remain anonymous.

10. The greater part of the selection is written in the form of a
   - ☐ a. political essay.
   - ☐ b. fictional account.
   - ☐ c. government report.
   - ☐ d. descriptive narrative.

Comprehension Skills Key

1. recalling specific facts
2. retaining concepts
3. organizing facts
4. understanding the main idea
5. drawing a conclusion
6. making a judgment
7. making an inference
8. recognizing tone
9. understanding characters
10. appreciating literary forms

VOCABULARY—PART TWO

Write the word that makes the most sense in each sentence.

abruptly	**imploringly**
mingled	**pitiable**
annihilate	

1. The city had remained the same for years, but then everything changed _____ .

2. A bomb left everything in ruins: it seemed to _____ the whole city.

3. Rich and poor alike _____ together crying in misery.

4. People buried beneath the rubble cried _____ for help.

5. The whole scene was so _____ that it would have driven an observer to tears.

pessimistic	**stimulates**
beneficial	**cistern**
obsessed	

6. A woman is hiding in a(n) _____ where a little clean water still remains.

7. This water can be _____ in keeping her alive for a while.

8. She tries not to be _____ , but there is little to feel good about.

9. She is _____ with worry about her sister's safety and can think of nothing else.

10. This worry finally _____ her to leave her hiding place and begin a search.

Comprehension [   ]

Vocabulary [   ]

UNDERSTANDING THROUGH WRITING

Pretend that you were a survivor of the bombing of Hiroshima. Write a letter to your American cousin describing your experiences. Use details from the story to make the scene come alive for your cousin.

_____

_____

_____

_____

_____

_____

_____

_____

BUILDING STUDY SKILLS

Read the following passage and answer the questions that follow it.

Mastering the Text, II

After checking on the author, it will be helpful to look at two of the standard features of a textbook, the table of contents and the bibliography.

1. Table of Contents. Next to the chapters themselves, this is the most important part of the book. It shows not only what is covered but also how the material is organized. If the subject is dealt with historically or chronologically, from its beginnings to the present, you know that the most current material will come at the end.

The author's approach may not be historical. For instance, if it is one that analyzes the subject, then simple, basic ideas will be presented early in the text. You will need to know and understand those if you are to grasp complex material presented later.

In examining the table of contents you can tell how the subject will be presented, even if you are not well versed in it. You may see listed in the table of contents a section that interests you. Prereading that section will add to your background in the subject area and may help you appreciate the rest of the material in the text.

2. The Bibliography. At the end of a textbook, you will usually find a bibliography, which is a list of other books that were used by the author as reference or source materials. That list can be a good indication of how the author put the book together. For instance, by reading the publication dates of the books listed, you can see if the author used both early and recent books on the subject. By examining the level of the sources you can judge if they are comprehensive or highly specialized. Perhaps you will even see a book cited that you will want to read for additional information.

1. The table of contents reveals the material covered in the book and how it is _____ .

2. Historical presentation proceeds from the _____ to the latest.

3. Analytical presentation proceeds from the simple to the _____ .

4. The bibliography is a list of books used by the author to obtain _____ on the subject.

5. A bibliography accompanying "Children of the A-Bomb" might list other articles on the American _____ of Hiroshima.

15

After Twenty Years

O. Henry

READING PURPOSE—
This selection describes the meeting of two long-separated friends. Read to see if you can predict how justice will play a part in their reunion.

VOCABULARY—PART ONE

All of these words are in the selection you are about to read. Study each word and its meaning. Then answer the questions below. As you read the selection, notice how each vocabulary word is used.

intricate: complex, puzzling

pacific: peaceful

stalwart: sturdy; strongly built

stanchest: most loyal (alternative spelling of *staunchest*)

dismally: sadly; gloomily

absurdity: something unreasonable or ridiculous

moderately: somewhat; rather

egotism: vanity; self-centeredness

submerged: covered over or hidden just below the surface

simultaneously: occurring at the same time

---

1. Which word names the quality of a person who constantly talks about himself and how well he does everything?

_____

2. Which word could describe a treasure chest that had been buried under the water?

_____

3. Which word could be used in describing how the phone and the doorbell rang at exactly the same moment?

_____

4. Which word might you use in describing a 1,500-piece puzzle consisting of only three colors?

_____

5. Which word might be considered an antonym for *very*?

_____

1   The policeman on the beat moved up the avenue impressively. The impressiveness was habitual and not for show, for spectators were few. The time was barely 10 o'clock at night, but chilly gusts of wind with a taste of rain in them had well nigh depeopled the streets.

2   Trying doors as he went, twirling his club with many <u>intricate</u> and artful movements, turning now and then to cast his watchful eye down the <u>pacific</u> thoroughfare, the officer, with his <u>stalwart</u> form and slight swagger, made a fine picture of a guardian of the peace. The vicinity was one that kept early hours. Now and then you might see the lights of a cigar store or of an all-night lunch counter; but the majority of the doors belonged to business places that had long since been closed.

3   When about midway of a certain block the policeman suddenly slowed his walk. In the doorway of a darkened hardware store a man leaned, with an unlighted cigar in his mouth. As the policeman walked up to him the man spoke up quickly.

4   "It's all right, officer," he said, reassuringly. "I'm just waiting for a friend. It's an appointment made twenty years ago. Sounds a little funny to you, doesn't it? Well, I'll explain if you'd like to make certain it's all straight. About that long ago there used to be a restaurant where this store stands—'Big Joe' Brady's restaurant."

5   "Until five years ago," said the policeman. "It was torn down then."

6   The man in the doorway struck a match and lit his cigar. The light showed a pale, square-jawed face with keen eyes, and a little white scar near his right eyebrow. His scarfpin was a large diamond, oddly set.

7   "Twenty years ago tonight," said the man, "I dined here at 'Big Joe' Brady's with Jimmy Wells, my best chum, and the finest chap in the world. He and I were raised here in New York, just like two brothers, together. I was eighteen and Jimmy was twenty. The next morning I was to start for the West to make my fortune. You couldn't have dragged Jimmy out of New York; he thought it was the only place on earth. Well, we agreed that night that we would meet here again exactly twenty years from that date and time, no matter what our conditions might be or from what distance we might have to come. We figured that in twenty years each of us ought to have our destiny worked out and our fortunes made, whatever they were going to be."

8   "It sounds pretty interesting," said the policeman. "Rather a long time between meets, though, it seems to me. Haven't you heard from your friend since you left?"

9   "Well, yes, for a time we corresponded," said the other. "But after a year or two we lost track of each other. You see, the West is a pretty big proposition, and I kept hustling around over it pretty lively. But I know Jimmy will meet me here if he's alive, for he always was the truest, <u>stanchest</u> old chap in the world. He'll never forget. I came a thousand miles to stand in this door tonight, and it's worth it if my old partner turns up."

10   The waiting man pulled out a handsome watch, the lids of it set with small diamonds.

11   "Three minutes to ten," he announced. "It was exactly ten o'clock when we parted here at the restaurant door."

12   "Did pretty well out West didn't you?" asked the policeman.

13   "You bet! I hope Jimmy has done half as well. He was a kind of plodder, though, good fellow as he was. I've had to compete with some of the sharpest wits going to get my pile. A man gets in a groove in New York. It takes the West to put a razor-edge on him."

14   The policeman twirled his club and took a step or two.

15   "I'll be on my way. Hope your friend comes around all right. Going to call time on him sharp?"

16   "I should say not!" said the other. "I'll give him half an hour at least. If Jimmy is alive on earth he'll be here by that time. So long, officer."

17   "Good-night, sir," said the policeman, passing on along his beat, trying doors as he went.

18   There was now a fine, cold drizzle falling, and the wind had risen from its uncertain puffs into a steady blow. The few foot passengers astir in that quarter hurried <u>dismally</u> and silently along with coat collars turned high and pocketed hands. And in the door of the hardware store the man who had come a thousand miles to fill an appointment, uncertain almost to <u>absurdity</u>, with the friend of his youth, smoked his cigar and waited.

19   About twenty minutes he waited, and then a tall man in a long overcoat, with collar turned up to his

ears, hurried across from the opposite side of the street. He went directly to the waiting man.

20 "Is that you, Bob?" he asked, doubtfully.

21 "Is that you, Jimmy Wells?" cried the man in the door.

22 "Bless my heart!" exclaimed the new arrival, grasping both the other's hands with his own "It's Bob, sure as fate. I was certain I'd find you here if you were still in existence. Well, well, well!—twenty years is a long time. The old restaurant's gone, Bob; I wish it had lasted, so we could have had another dinner there. How has the West treated you, old man?"

23 "Bully; it has given me everything I asked it for. You've changed lots, Jimmy. I never thought you were so tall by two or three inches."

24 "Oh, I grew a bit after I was twenty."

25 "Doing well in New York, Jimmy?"

26 "<u>Moderately</u>. I have a position in one of the city departments. Come on, Bob; we'll go around to a place I know of, and have a good long talk about old times."

27 The two men started up the street, arm in arm. The man from the West, his <u>egotism</u> enlarged by success, was beginning to outline the history of his career. The other, <u>submerged</u> in his overcoat, listened with interest.

28 At the corner stood a drug store, brilliant with electric lights. When they came into this glare each of them turned <u>simultaneously</u> to gaze upon the other's face.

29 The man from the West stopped suddenly and released his arm.

30 "You're not Jimmy Wells," he snapped. "Twenty years is a long time, but not long enough to change a man's nose from a Roman to a pug."

"In the door of the hardware store the man who had come a thousand miles to fill an appointment…smoked his cigar and waited."

31 "It sometimes changes a good man into a bad one," said the tall man. "You've been under arrest for ten minutes, 'Silky' Bob. Chicago thinks you may have dropped over our way and wires us she wants to have a chat with you. Going quietly, are you? That's sensible. Now, before we go to the station here's a note I was asked to hand to you. You may read it here at the window. It's from Patrolman Wells."

32 The man from the West unfolded the little piece of paper handed him. His hand was steady when he began to read, but it trembled a little by the time he had finished. The note was rather short.

33 *Bob: I was at the appointed place on time. When you struck the match to light your cigar I saw it was the face of the man wanted in Chicago. Somehow I couldn't do it myself, so I went around and got a plain clothes man to do the job.*

Jimmy

Starting Time	
Finishing Time	
Reading Time	
Reading Rate	

COMPREHENSION

Read the following questions and statements. For each one, put an X in the box before the option that contains the most complete or accurate answer.

1. This story takes place in
   - ☐ a. Chicago.
   - ☐ b. New York.
   - ☐ c. Kansas City.
   - ☐ d. the West.

2. Bob and Jimmy's meeting is intended to be
   - ☐ a. a time for Jimmy to invest in Bob's company.
   - ☐ b. a time for Bob to turn himself in.
   - ☐ c. a reunion.
   - ☐ d. a dinner meeting that they have every year.

3. The surprise element in this story is that
   - ☐ a. it is set on a cold, rainy night.
   - ☐ b. Bob has gotten rich in the West.
   - ☐ c. Bob is not arrested immediately.
   - ☐ d. the policeman is really Jimmy.

4. Which of the following sayings best sums up the point of this story?
   - ☐ a. People who live in glass houses shouldn't throw stones.
   - ☐ b. Slow but steady wins the race.
   - ☐ c. Monkey see, monkey do.
   - ☐ d. A stitch in time saves nine.

5. When Bob first saw Jimmy, he
   - ☐ a. did not recognize his friend.
   - ☐ b. recognized Jimmy, but pretended he didn't.
   - ☐ c. hid in the doorway because Jimmy was a policeman.
   - ☐ d. decided not to talk to him.

6. An early clue that the plain clothes policeman is not Jimmy is that
   - ☐ a. he doesn't remember 'Big Joe' Brady's restaurant.
   - ☐ b. he is wearing a diamond scarfpin.
   - ☐ c. he is taller than Bob remembers Jimmy being.
   - ☐ d. he has a pug nose.

7. When Jimmy writes in paragraph 33, "Somehow I couldn't do it myself," he means that
   - ☐ a. he would feel bad about arresting his old friend.
   - ☐ b. arrests of famous criminals should be done by plain clothes men.
   - ☐ c. he was afraid that Bob would try to kill him.
   - ☐ d. he wants Bob sent directly to Chicago.

8. When Bob talks about his life, the tone he uses is one of
   - ☐ a. regret.
   - ☐ b. bragging.
   - ☐ c. humbleness.
   - ☐ d. politeness.

9. Which of the following best describes Jimmy's feelings about his job?
   - ☐ a. It is not as important as friendship.
   - ☐ b. It proves that he has does just as well as Bob has.
   - ☐ c. He would like it better if he were a plain clothes man.
   - ☐ d. It is more important to him than anything else.

10. For men like Bob, the West is a symbol of
    - ☐ a. opportunity and excitement.
    - ☐ b. poverty and despair.
    - ☐ c. glamour and sophistication.
    - ☐ d. steadiness and plodding.

Comprehension Skills Key

1. recalling specific facts
2. retaining concepts
3. organizing facts
4. understanding the main idea
5. drawing a conclusion
6. making a judgment
7. making an inference
8. recognizing tone
9. understanding characters
10. appreciating literary forms

VOCABULARY—PART TWO

Write the word that makes the most sense in each sentence.

pacific　　　　**stalwart**
stanchest　　　**moderately**
egotism

1. Bob thought he was pretty important; in fact, his

   _____ was his most noticeable

   quality.

2. He particularly remembered Jimmy's loyalty,

   calling him the _____ of men.

3. Jimmy was not the chief of police, but he had

   done _____ well at his job.

4. He was a(n) _____ man who

   looked as if he could easily overpower most

   criminals.

5. But even though he could get angry when neces-

   sary, at heart Jimmy had a _____

   temperament.

submerged　　　**simultaneously**
intricate　　　　**dismally**
absurdity

6. Figuring out how to arrest Bob was a(n)

   _____ problem requiring much

   thought.

7. Jimmy clearly realized the _____

   of having to arrest his best friend.

8. Just underneath his devotion to duty were

   _____ feelings of loyalty to Bob.

9. If he and Bob had recognized each other

   _____ , Bob might have been

   able to talk him out of it.

10. But unfortunately, he had recognized Bob first,

    and so he _____ went about his

    sad duty.

Comprehension [　　　　　]

Vocabulary [　　　　　]

UNDERSTANDING THROUGH WRITING

Was it right of Jimmy to arrest his old friend? Why or why not? Write your ideas in a paragraph or two. If you think Jimmy was not right, tell what you think he should have done instead.

_____

_____

_____

_____

_____

_____

_____

_____

_____

_____

BUILDING STUDY SKILLS

Read the following passage and answer the questions that follow it.

Mastering the Text, III

Another feature of the text you will want to explore is the index. Use it to obtain hard facts about the author and his or her presentation.

The Index. Every textbook contains a subject index. There may be other indexes too. An authors index, for example, may allow you to look up by name those writers mentioned throughout the book. The index will also list their writings and works.

But the subject index is likely to be the only one included in your texts. It lists alphabetically topics that were discussed in the text. The page number is given with each listing.

Based on classroom lectures or on some previous knowledge of yours about the subject area, examine an author's treatment of one topic. First, look through the index until you find a familiar entry. Then go to the page listed and read the material. What kind of job has the author done with it? Did he or she discuss what you expected? Was the treatment too general? Make more checks if needed to see if the treatment is the same throughout the book. You may find that the text covers the field with more depth than you need; or, the opposite may be the case—the text is too sketchy for you. You may need to find a book that gives a more comprehensive treatment.

Of course, you may be unable to change texts and authors. The text you have may be the book assigned for the course. But you can use other texts. If needed, find one to supplement the one you think is lacking something, one that you can read first to make the assigned text easier to understand. Or you may wish to read a more extensive text, along with the assigned one, to broaden your knowledge. In other words, feed your interest in the subject—find a text that works for you and keeps your interest level high.

1. A subject index lists _____ in alphabetical order.

2. For example, in a collection of stories, "After Twenty Years" might be indexed under "stories with _____ endings."

3. Each listing in an index is given with a page _____ .

4. As a check, see how the author treats a subject with which you are _____ .

5. If the text does not completely suit your needs, you may wish to _____ it with another.

TOPIC REVIEW
React to Topic 3

Respond to one or more of these questions as your instructor directs.

1. Both Shao Ching and Elise Radell were victims of injustice. What was similar about their situations? What was different? Make a list of the similarities and differences. Include at least three of each in your list.

\
\
\
\
\
\

2. Using the list you developed in question 1, write a paragraph or two comparing and contrasting Shao Ching and Elise Radell.

\
\
\
\
\
\

3. In Building Study Skills 12 you learned about Counter Signals, words or phrases that signal a reversal in thought. Counter Signals are used often in "Children of the A-Bomb," selection 14. Review the selection and find at least four different Counter Signals in it. Write the sentences they occur in and tell how each one changes the meaning of the thought that precedes it.

\
\
\
\

4. Choose a character from "The Cow-Tail Switch" or from "After Twenty Years" that might think he received unjust treatment from someone else in the story. Write a short speech that this character might present, beginning with the words "I was treated unfairly because…" In the speech, give the reasons why the character might feel he was badly treated. Make the speech sound the way you think the character would talk. Then be ready to present your speech to a group of fellow students.

_____

_____

_____

_____

_____

5. The events described in "Children of the A-Bomb" and "Then Came the Famous *Kristallnacht*" happened in the middle part of the twentieth century. How likely is it that such events could occur today? Write your opinion, and then explain the reasons for it. Be sure to refer to specific things that happened in the two selections as you talk about what might happen today.

_____

_____

_____

_____

_____

_____

_____

6. Jimmy is portrayed in "After Twenty Years" as a strong, silent type of policeman. Is this the way police officers are usually characterized in television shows? Think of two or three officers in shows you watch. Write short descriptions of the kind of people they are. Show the ways they are or are not like Jimmy.

_____

_____

_____

_____

_____

_____

In Nature there are neither rewards nor punishments—there are consequences.

—Robert Ingersoll (1833–1899)

FACING THE ELEMENTS

16

The Day I Nearly Drowned

June Mellies Reno

READING PURPOSE—
In this selection a woman faces a strong possibility of drowning. Read to find out what gives her the will to survive.

VOCABULARY—PART ONE

All of these words are in the selection you are about to read. Study each word and its meaning. Then answer the questions below. As you read the selection, notice how each vocabulary word is used.

elected: chose

immensity: hugeness; vastness

prudence: caution; common sense

meek: humble; timid

futile: useless

despairingly: without hope

interval: period of time

soothe: comfort; make calm

indignantly: in a manner expressing strong displeasure at something unfair

adrenalin: hormone that increases bodily energy by speeding up the heartbeat

1. Which word names the quality you would be displaying if you carried an umbrella on an overcast day?

_____

2. Which word could describe a person who is afraid to speak up for herself even when she is criticized?

_____

3. Which word might you use in discussing the size of an ocean?

_____

4. Which word could be an antonym for *useful*?

_____

5. Which word might describe what a father is doing if he holds, pats, and hugs a crying baby?

_____

1   A few summers ago I nearly drowned. But I'm alive today (and glad of it!) because of a lovely blonde woman who doesn't exist.

2   It all happened when friends invited us to spend a week with them at Amagansett on the south shore of Long Island. We found bright, sunny weather the day we arrived, but a stiff breeze and unusually high tides. A recent storm had chopped away the gentle slope of the beach and each wave thundered in against a wall of hard-packed sand.

3   In order for our four children and our hosts' three to bathe safely, we adults backed into the low surf and, clasping hands, formed a human chain. Within that safeguard the children frolicked and when one of them got bowled over there was always someone ready to grab hold.

4   The youngsters swam in the morning. Then, while the smaller ones were napping and the older ones reading, it was adult swim time.

5   That afternoon I <u>elected</u> to stay behind for an hour in order to catch up on laundry that had piled up during a two-week camping trip we had taken before coming to Long Island. When I had the clothes flapping on the line I sprinted for the beach. My husband had already had his dip and was snoozing on a big beach towel. I blew him a kiss as I passed him and splashed into the surf. The other members of the party were still swimming.

6   "You're late!" one said.

7   "True," I replied, "but we needed some clean underwear!"

8   A few minutes later the other swimmers said they'd had enough and turned toward the shore. They left me out beyond the surfline, alone. No one worried, least of all me. I was a Red Cross lifesaver and I had swum in heavy surf all my life. Also, when I was in college I had served on the Mississippi River Patrol, an organization of trained swimmers who specialized in pulling the foolhardy out of whirlpools. I, of course, knew and had often taught the Red Cross maxim which says that nobody…should swim alone.

9   But I had frequently ignored this common-sense warning—I liked the feeling of being alone in the <u>immensity</u> of God's great ocean, and I was confident of my ability to take care of myself in the water. Now I splashed around by myself, turning on my back to watch the gulls swooping low over the gray-blue swells.

10   Then, having enjoyed my brief period of solitude, I started to head back in to join my husband and friends on the beach. I was about 200 feet from shore in 15 feet of water. I flung a look over my shoulder, saw a good-sized wave coming I could ride in on, and tried to climb on top of it.

11   To this day I don't know if I was ahead of that wave or behind the next one. All I know is, suddenly, in a few seconds' time, I was rolled and slammed—hard—against the sandy bottom. I surfaced, now only about 50 feet from the beach, angry at the wave and annoyed with myself for having miscalculated so badly. I swam back out to mount another wave, made another poorly timed try, and hit the ocean floor again. This time I scraped my knee painfully on an undersea rock, but I tried again—and was promptly rolled again.

12   I don't panic easily, but a small alarm went off in the back of my brain. It said something like, "Okay, smart alec, you are in a bit of trouble."

13   The problem was that the surf in those last hundred feet or so was just too rough to swim through to the shore. I *had* to ride through it on a wave, but they were churning too violently and were breaking too far short of the beach. The water was still too deep for me to get solid footing and the undertow was so strong it kept dragging me down to the bottom.

14   "Never swim alone." I had taught that lesson to hundreds of swimmers—including my own children—but here I was, alone and in what could develop into an extremely dangerous situation. I remembered one of the basic rules for surf swimmers: "If you find you can't get into shore, turn around and swim out where the water is calmer. There you can catch your breath and make some new plans." That is what I did.

15   Back where I started, I had a clear view of the beach and of my husband and friends all apparently sound asleep and probably beyond earshot. No action could be expected from them.

16   Now the wind was brisker and I was swimming through whitecaps. The waves were higher; the tide was incoming and surging. A short distance away I knew there was a public beach where husky lifeguards were on duty. I lingered a moment, treading water, torn between <u>prudence</u> and pride. The idea of being hauled out of the water by a lifeguard was humiliating—after all, *I* was a lifeguard!

17   Just then an oversized whitecap hit me smack in the face. I swallowed what seemed like a quart of salt water, and almost immediately I felt a nagging pain in my stomach. I felt dizzy and nauseous and

very cold. It was time, I knew, to ask for help—in a dignified way, of course.

18 Feeling <u>meek</u> I turned around and started swimming toward the public beach, which I estimated to be about a half mile away—not far on a calm day, but quite a distance in heavy seas.

19 When I got there, finally, my heart fell. The beach was deserted! The life-

"A huge wave carried me in nearer, nearer, then turned me over. I was seized by a terribly powerful force and rolled around and around underwater."

guard's chair was empty and there was a big red sign planted in front of it that said, "No Swimming Today—Dangerous Conditions."

20 By the time I had struggled the half mile back to Amagansett, gasping against wind and tide, I was really tired. When I saw my husband and our friends yawning and stretching and beginning to sit up, my pride and vanity vanished completely.

21 "Hey, Bob! Ted!" I yelled. "Help!"

22 But it was <u>futile</u>; the offshore wind was carrying my voice toward South America.

23 "I couldn't be drowning—not me!" I thought with a growing sense of surprise and annoyance. I stiffened my body into a human surfboard and made another try for shore. A huge wave carried me in nearer, nearer, then turned me over. I was seized by a terribly powerful force and rolled around and around under water. I ate sand, cut my lip on pebbles, felt slippery seaweed twine around my arms, then tear away.

24 There is no ocean swimmer who has not, at one time or another, felt the fearsome tug of an undertow, that strange counter-current that push-pulls you down to destruction. *Webster's Dictionary* describes it as a "current beneath the waves." Far better swimmers than I have drowned in it. I tried to break through it to reach the beach, but the more I struggled, the deeper I got into the pull of the undertow. Now I couldn't get into the beach—and I couldn't get out again either! I was whirling like a stray sock in a washing machine.

25 I tried to force myself to be calm and remember what I'd been told to do if caught in an undertow:

Do not fight against the cross currents. Go limp. Protect your head by crossing your arms over it. You will come to the surface every instant or so. Concentrate on getting a breath then. Signal for help, if you can. An extra big wave may toss you up onshore. The wind may change, the tide turn and you may be carried out of the whirlpool. Someone may come to get you. Hang on and hope for the best.

26 I did all that for what seemed like quite a long time, but I was getting extremely tired. I knew that even my ability to stick my head out of the water and grab a lungful of air wasn't going to last much longer. <u>Despairingly</u> I cast a glance at the beach, which wasn't much farther away than the length of my living room.

27 I was drowning less than 50 feet from shore. Ridiculous. It was just a short walk to safety, to my husband and children. Now my arms, which had been rigidly crossed above my head to protect it from the rocks, floated loosely by my side. I let go.

28 "You are drowning," I told myself drowsily. "Isn't it lovely?" The thought which had seemed so terrifying now seemed strangely delicious. I opened my eyes and in those blue-green depths something very soft and inviting reached out to me. I had a vision of myself standing in a white marble court explaining things to a large and disapproving angel who seemed to be the judge.

29 "Your Honor," I admitted, "I had too much vanity." Then I added, "And pride."

30 Other near-drowned persons have testified to the last-moment flash that occurs as you go down and out. Nurses in hospitals have observed that dying patients suddenly become brilliantly alert in their last few mortal minutes. On the bottom of the Atlantic Ocean it happened to me. My fantasy ended. My mind turned on like a high-voltage computer.

31 "My family!" the message chattered frantically. "What will happen to my family?"

32 And in the same instant another very cool voice in my brain supplied the answer: "Well, your husband will be lonely. The children will need a mother. Your husband is attractive and successful; he will remarry—after a decent <u>interval</u>, of course."

33 "Who? Who will he marry?"

34 "No one you know," the message sought to <u>soothe</u> me. "But a nice person. Don't worry."

35 Then suddenly I saw her. She had lovely light blonde hair, not dishwater blonde like mine; she was ten years younger and ten pounds lighter. And she was standing in the doorway of my house with her arms around my children as she smilingly watched my handsome, adorable husband come up the driveway at the end of a day's work. It was all hers now!

36 "Why, the hussy!" I thought <u>indignantly</u>. "She's got a lot of nerve! I'll be gosh darned if I…." A burst of pure rage swept through me and with it, undoubtedly, a good shot of life-saving <u>adrenalin</u>. I planted my feet on the ocean floor, pushed hard and surfaced straight up like a dolphin. I found myself face to face with my host, Bob, who had noticed the roughening surf and had come out to look for me.

37 "Jump!" he shouted as another wave towered.

38 "I can't!" I gasped. He grabbed me and heaved me over his head neatly on top of the oncoming wave. I was washed up onto the beach like a piece of driftwood. Weakly I crawled through the foaming shallow water onto the dry, warm sand and collapsed in my husband's arms.

39 Still a big groggy from his nap, he hauled me to my feet and wrapped me in a big towel. He looked as blessedly solid as a dock piling, and I clung to him. After making sure I was all right, he began to scold me.

40 "Foolish!" he said. "Nobody's swimming on ten miles of this beach but you. And, besides, you know better than to go swimming *alone*! Who do you think you are?"

41 "Your wife," I choked gratefully. "I'll have 'never swim alone' tattooed on my…Oh, Honey, I love you!"

42 Later I tried to thank my rescuer for his help. He was offhand about it, knowing that one lifesaver doesn't embarrass another. "Looked like you could use a tow," was all he said.

43 And, of course, I'll never be able to thank the beautiful, mysterious blonde woman who helped to save my life. In fact, I hope she stays on the bottom of the Atlantic Ocean where she belongs—and that the rest of us have enough sense to stay on top.

Starting Time	
Finishing Time	
Reading Time	
Reading Rate	

COMPREHENSION

Read the following questions and statements. For each one, put an X in the box before the option that contains the most complete or accurate answer.

1. As the author was drowning, she had a vision of
   - ☐ a. an angel.
   - ☐ b. a blonde woman.
   - ☐ c. her own funeral.
   - ☐ d. her children dressed in black.

2. The narrator was a
   - ☐ a. newcomer to strong currents and heavy surf.
   - ☐ b. careful and prudent swimmer.
   - ☐ c. strong, experienced swimmer.
   - ☐ d. former professional swimming instructor.

3. The author first realized she was in trouble
   - ☐ a. after hitting the ocean bottom three times.
   - ☐ b. when she saw that the public beach was closed.
   - ☐ c. while shouting to her friends on the beach.
   - ☐ d. when she felt a pain in her stomach.

4. The purpose of the selection is to
   - ☐ a. entertain but also instruct.
   - ☐ b. impress and amuse.
   - ☐ c. inform but also frighten.
   - ☐ d. alarm and discourage.

5. Which of the following combinations of conditions presents a serious threat to bathers?
   - ☐ a. long waves and a sandy bottom
   - ☐ b. high tides and distance swimming
   - ☐ c. low tides and high winds
   - ☐ d. rough surf and strong undertow

6. The decision to form a human chain was a
   - ☐ a. good idea.
   - ☐ b. foolish idea.
   - ☐ c. calculated risk.
   - ☐ d. childish impulse.

7. The ocean, in all of its moods, should be considered with
   - ☐ a. fear.
   - ☐ b. respect.
   - ☐ c. suspicion.
   - ☐ d. trust.

8. The underlying tone of the selection is
   - ☐ a. serious.
   - ☐ b. casual.
   - ☐ c. humorous.
   - ☐ d. mysterious.

9. Bob was
   - ☐ a. considerate.
   - ☐ b. forgetful.
   - ☐ c. timid.
   - ☐ d. indecisive.

10. Two examples of alliteration can be found in the selection:
    - ☐ a. chattered frantically; thought indignantly.
    - ☐ b. hard-packed sand; gray-blue swells.
    - ☐ c. rigidly crossed; promptly rolled.
    - ☐ d. vanity vanished; mortal minutes.

Comprehension Skills Key

1. recalling specific facts	6. making a judgment
2. retaining concepts	7. making an inference
3. organizing facts	8. recognizing tone
4. understanding the main idea	9. understanding characters
5. drawing a conclusion	10. appreciating literary forms

VOCABULARY—PART TWO

Write the word that makes the most sense in each sentence.

interval	elected
soothe	immensity
prudence	

1. If the woman in the story had more _____ , she wouldn't have gotten herself into the dangerous situation she was in.

2. Rather than stay with her companions, she had _____ to swim out alone.

3. The _____ of the ocean did not trouble her; to her it was just like a bathtub.

4. For a short _____ she was safe, but it was not long before she ran into trouble.

5. She tried to _____ herself with reminders that she was an excellent swimmer.

indignantly	meek
adrenalin	futile
despairingly	

6. After trying unsuccessfully to get to shore, she began to realize that her efforts were _____ .

7. She paddled around _____ , with no hope of getting out alive.

8. No longer a fighter, she had almost turned into a _____ person waiting to drown.

9. But she reacted quite _____ at the thought that her husband would quickly forget her.

10. A burst of _____ pushed her on, and she was able to reach land safely.

Comprehension [ ]

Vocabulary [ ]

UNDERSTANDING THROUGH WRITING

Think of a situation where adrenalin helped you do something you felt too weak or afraid to do. Write a short description of what happened. Be sure to explain how your feelings changed as you suddenly became stronger.

_____

_____

_____

_____

_____

_____

_____

_____

BUILDING STUDY SKILLS

Read the following passage and answer the questions that follow it.

Mastering the Text, IV

You know from earlier discussions that previewing is the first step in reading. Fortunately, the organization of today's textbooks makes previewing quick and rewarding. Listed below are the steps to follow when previewing a textbook chapter.

1. Read the Title. As pointed out earlier, the title is the author's announcement of what is to come. It may in fact define the limits of the entire chapter.

2. Read the Subheads. The subheads may list the author's three or four main points. They also may give a clue to the significance of the forthcoming material. In either case, reading the subheads will give you a jump on the chapter.

3. Read the Illustrations. Don't just look at the illustrations; read them. The role of graphs, maps, and charts is to present visually information that might otherwise take hundreds of words to cover. Graphic aids often demonstrate a relationship between two facts. That relationship may be the very heart of the chapter—the base upon which the entire discussion is founded. Skipping over such obviously important aids in the name of saving time can decrease understanding. That in turn increases the time it takes to comprehend the material completely.

4. Read the Opening Paragraph. This helps you organize the material to come. Try to see what will be expected of you as you read.

5. Read the Closing Paragraph. Capitalize on the author's parting words, the statements that cap the chapter.

6. Skim Through the Chapter. Get the feel of the presentation. Use typographical aids such as roman numerals, headlines, italics, and capital letters. Try to pick out the three or four main points to be covered. In that way, the sense of the lesson will be apparent to you even before you study it.

1. The title and _____ of a chapter will give you an idea of what the chapter covers.

2. Visual aids can help you quickly grasp information that it might take hundreds of _____ to cover.

3. For instance, the photo of strong waves accompanying this selection should have helped you understand the _____ that the woman swimmer was in.

4. Read the opening and _____ paragraphs to give you a better understanding of the material's scope.

5. The opening and closing paragraphs of this article should have encouraged you to skim for more information on the mysterious _____ .

Autumn Storm

Faith McNulty

VOCABULARY—PART ONE

All of these words are in the selection you are about to read. Study each word and its meaning. Then answer the questions below. As you read the selection, notice how each vocabulary word is used.

queue: line

beset: worried; troubled

foreboding: feeling that something bad will happen

dire: very bad; dreadful

unprecedented: rare; remarkable

assailed: attacked

lore: traditional facts or beliefs

intact: in one piece

vanguard: front; foremost part of

imminent: about to happen immediately

---

1. Which word describes the condition of a glass that falls to the floor but does not break?

   _____

2. Which word could describe your feeling that a terrible fight will break out at your class reunion tomorrow?

   _____

3. Which word describes an event that is going to occur in the next minute or two?

   _____

4. Which word might be used in talking about the stories, customs, and beliefs that have always been part of a family?

   _____

5. Which word might describe a surprising event that you had never seen happen before?

   _____

1   I am writing this before the hurricane, on an electric typewriter. After the storm, this typewriter won't work. It is 9:30 P.M., and the six o'clock news said the storm was coming straight at us. My husband and I have spent all day on the storm. By about six o'clock, we had done everything we could, and were very tired. In the morning, when we first heard that the storm was coming our way, we thought about food and light and fuel, but without any sense of real urgency. Then we drove to town around noon and found that our gas station had a <u>queue</u> of cars, stretching out into the highway. In an instant, the psychology of shortage <u>beset</u> us. We drew up at the end of the line, wondering if the gas would hold out until we got to it. It did. We drove on, and found, to our surprise, that the hardware store was open, thought today is a legal holiday here—V-J Day. Al Damon, the proprietor, had opened the store because of the storm, and was alone behind the counter in semi-darkness. We joined a huddle of people waiting to ask for hurricane lanterns, fuel, charcoal, candles. Damon handed out the supplies on his shelves and then went down into the basement and brought up all he had. With his permission, we telephoned a couple of friends and told them of the opportunity. When our turn came, we asked for four lanterns—the extra lanterns were for our friends. Next, we picked up the mail, and I was struck by how faithfully we performed this habitual errand, which could not possibly have anything to do with the coming night—the night the big ash tree might fall.

2   The big ash tree. That is at the heart of my <u>foreboding</u>. From the moment I remembered the tree—while we waited for our loot of lamps and charcoal—I have been aware of how terrible it will be if the ash tree falls. The ash tree is about ninety feet tall and about ninety feet wide. A tree man came by once and said that it must be at least two hundred years old. It is so big you can't see how big it is until you get right up to the trunk and imagine climbing into the lowest branches. They are as high above you as the second story of a house and are as big around as ordinary tree trunks. A few years ago, one branch fell. It was a small part of the tree, but it lay spread out on the ground like a dead whale. My husband spent days cutting it up. The ash tree is between our house and our barn. If it falls westward, it will crash into our roof. If it falls toward the northeast, it could crush the barn. But it is not these <u>dire</u> possibilities that bother me. It is the thought that it might fall at all that I cannot bear.

3   We made a list of things to do. Draw water in bathtubs, fill gallon jugs with drinking water, check window latches, and so on. Our sins of omission have all been uncovered—the unfixed leaks, the unhinged screens. All day long, I have been conscious of using things that perhaps will not be here, or usable, tomorrow. Hot water from the faucet. The electric stove, on which I boiled a dozen eggs. The electric clock. I stifled an impulse to vacuum the floors—for me, an <u>unprecedented</u> desire. When the kitchen was tidy, we worked outdoors, dragging in the porch furniture, picking up every odd tool or object that might hurtle through a window. Most of the day, rain fell straight down—warm and needle-fine or warm and in fat streams, as though from an adjustable shower head. I often looked at the sky, where I supposed the sword of Damocles hung concealed in the wads of dark gray cloud folded over us. There was almost no wind—strangely little wind for such a lot of rain. Between showers, a great many swallows appeared and swooped and dived and rose again, as though very excited.

4   The pleasantest thing I did all day was to prepare our two horses for the night ahead. I cleaned the stalls, brought in fresh bedding and buckets of clean water, and filled the racks with hay. The horses were probably amazed, because in summer I don't usually do anything like this for them but leave them out to take care of themselves. They were very wet, and entered the stalls willingly and ate the hay with a look of gratification. When I closed the doors of their stable, the small dwelling looked quite secure. It was the only thing I had done all day that I felt might really turn out all right.

5   By six o'clock, everything was done, and everything outside was quiet. Inside, there was the TV—the news programs full of alarms, and charts showing the storm coming, and pictures of people hauling in their boats and leaving their homes. A sudden lonesomeness <u>assailed</u> me. Earlier in the day, I had made one or two essential phone calls, but I hadn't had time for anything else. Now I began to call friends. A number of lines were busy. We were establishing communications. Tomorrow, phoning will probably be

impossible. Like us, several friends live at the end of long, tree-lined roads and very likely will not get their cars out for days, until the debris of fallen trees is cleared. We decided to leave our car out on the highway, a quarter of a mile from the house. I called my friends and arranged to go by tomorrow

"All day long, I have been conscious of using things that most perhaps will not be here, or usable, tomorrow."

many hurricanes, but now, in its great age, it is more vulnerable than ever before. There was nothing else I could do for it, so I pronounced a blessing on it, as though it were going into a battle. Its multitude of leaves reminded me of a medieval host. Its lashing arms seemed full of life and strength,

morning and look in their mailboxes, which are on the highway, so that if they have needs or messages for the outside world they can walk down their driveways and leave me a note. I was quite pleased at having thought of this simple way to survive the loss of the telephone. We exchanged hurricane lore. The heavy rain, we agree, increases the danger that trees will fall, because their roots can be more easily wrenched out of the softened earth. We discussed our nerves. We all hate waiting. "Are you nervous?" someone asks. "I've been nervous as a cat all day."

6   Just before dark, I went out and picked all the flowers—begonias, nicotiana, zinnias, well washed but still <u>intact</u>. I gathered an armful, in profusion. I looked at my dozen of green tomatoes and wondered if they would survive. There was still no wind.

7   Now we're battened down. There is no one else to call. We've had supper. The TV news says the storm is coming, but here inside the lighted house there is no sign of anything unusual, except the sound of leaves. A few minutes ago, I stepped outside and found that it was still warm—seventy-two degrees on the porch thermometer. The air was very soft, but there was no rain. The wind felt gentle and smelled sweet and tropical, alien to New England. Whereas all day we'd had the sound of dripping rain, now we had the sound of leaves stirring. The <u>vanguard</u> of the storm has arrived. I looked up into the branches of the monumental ash tree. They were moving restlessly, as though the tree were coming to life to meet the <u>imminent</u> struggle. It must have lived through

and I returned to the house with new hope that the green ash would be there in the morning.

Starting Time	
Finishing Time	
Reading Time	
Reading Rate	

COMPREHENSION

Read the following questions and statements. For each one, put an X in the box before the option that contains the most complete or accurate answer.

1. The hurricane is expected to hit
   ☐ a. in the morning.
   ☐ b. around noon.
   ☐ c. in the late afternoon.
   ☐ d. at night.

2. The area that the author lives in is
   ☐ a. out in the country.
   ☐ b. along a deserted beach.
   ☐ c. in a big city.
   ☐ d. in the suburbs of a big city.

3. The time frame of this selection
   - ☐ a. begins at night and flashes back to what happened all day.
   - ☐ b. starts in the morning and ends in the evening.
   - ☐ c. covers two days, from morning till night.
   - ☐ d. includes only two hours in an afternoon.

4. This selection is mostly about
   - ☐ a. buying supplies.
   - ☐ b. remembering the past.
   - ☐ c. preparing for the worst.
   - ☐ d. comforting one's friends.

5. The author worries about the ash tree falling mostly because
   - ☐ a. it could make a huge hole in her roof.
   - ☐ b. it could destroy her barn.
   - ☐ c. she would not want to see it die.
   - ☐ d. it is already half dead.

6. In paragraph 5 the writer is overcome by a "sudden lonesomeness" because
   - ☐ a. she is alone in the house.
   - ☐ b. she needs the comfort of talking to others who are in the same situation.
   - ☐ c. she is sure the tree will fall.
   - ☐ d. she feels bad that the horses have to go through the storm by themselves.

7. The "sweet and tropical" smell of the wind described in paragraph 7 suggests that
   - ☐ a. the storm won't be that serious.
   - ☐ b. only tropical trees like palms will remain standing.
   - ☐ c. the writer is looking forward to the storm.
   - ☐ d. the storm is moving in from the south.

8. The overall feeling conveyed in this selection is one of
   - ☐ a. anger.
   - ☐ b. denial.
   - ☐ c. loneliness.
   - ☐ d. anticipation.

9. The author of this selection comes across as
   - ☐ a. nervous and highstrung.
   - ☐ b. calm and accepting of fate.
   - ☐ c. very unsure of herself.
   - ☐ d. more worried about her husband than herself.

10. The description of a branch of the tree "spread out on the ground like a dead whale" contains
    - ☐ a. personification.
    - ☐ b. a simile.
    - ☐ c. a metaphor.
    - ☐ d. alliteration.

Comprehension Skills Key

1. recalling specific facts
2. retaining concepts
3. organizing facts
4. understanding the main idea
5. drawing a conclusion
6. making a judgment
7. making an inference
8. recognizing tone
9. understanding characters
10. appreciating literary forms

VOCABULARY—PART TWO

Write the word that makes the most sense in each sentence.

queue	beset
dire	unprecedented
intact	

1. A hurricane strike was _____ : nothing like this had happened before in the area.

2. If the hurricane actually hit, the situation could quickly become very _____ .

3. Concern over having enough supplies _____ the people.

4. For example, a long _____ of people waited patiently to buy bottled water.

5. Many feared that their homes would not remain _____ under the force of the storm.

assailed   lore
foreboding   vanguard
imminent

6. A sense of _____ spread through the community as the skies darkened.

7. The _____ of the storm was announced by a sudden increase in the wind.

8. It _____ even the hugest trees till it seemed they would snap like twigs.

9. When the woman heard a loud crack overhead, she knew it signaled the _____ fall of a large branch.

10. This storm was so memorable that it quickly became part of the _____ of the community.

Comprehension [ ]

Vocabulary [ ]

UNDERSTANDING THROUGH WRITING

Decide whether the ash tree described in the selection will fall or survive the storm. Then pretend you are the author of the selection. Write a description of what happens to the tree. Make your description as vivid as you can.

_____

_____

_____

_____

_____

_____

_____

_____

_____

_____

BUILDING STUDY SKILLS

Read the following passage and answer the questions that follow it.

Marking the Text

If you own your textbook you will want to write in it. Marking the text as you read is creative reading—it is motivating and stimulating. It can be the most creative reading you do.

Don't make the mistake of some students—that of frequent highlighting. Many students feel that they should highlight important facts and information. But as they read, almost everything they encounter seems to be important. If you look at a book owned by a student who has this habit, you will find that almost a third of every chapter is marked. The highlighting is so distracting that the eye actually seeks out the unmarked passages.

So highlight selectively. Mark only passages that are of extreme importance, and use some other methods of marking the text that are effective and not distracting. For instance, to set off an important line or passage, use the abbreviation *imp.* in the margin. You can also use circles, numbers, and brackets.

Brackets are used in much the same way as highlighting. Look for and bracket important statements at the beginning of each new division. A strong summary statement is a good candidate for bracketing, too. But use brackets sparingly.

Circles and numbers are used to indicate important series and lists. Circle the key word that begins the series; then number the items in the series. This will help you to find the list later. Many times explanations and details accompany a list, and the items may be sentences, paragraphs, or even chapters apart.

Abbreviations are used as shown: to indicate the principal statement (*imp.*) of the whole lesson; a major illustration (*ill.*) that helps the reader understand an essential concept; and a conclusion (*con.*) based on facts and data included in the chapter.

1. Marking the text as you read can be the most _____ reading that you do.

2. Highlighting, if used _____ , can help you remember passages of extreme importance.

3. For instance, if you were trying to get a sense of what worried author Faith McNulty the most, you might highlight the first _____ sentences in paragraph 2.

4. _____ may be used to mark off statements and the beginning and end of each division.

5. Circle key words; and _____ the items in a series.

Into Thin Air

Jon Krakauer

READING PURPOSE—
This selection describes a mountain climber's descent from the Balcony, an area near the top of the world's highest mountain, Mt. Everest. Read to learn about the struggle it took for him to make the descent.

VOCABULARY—PART ONE

All of these words are in the selection you are about to read. Study each word and its meaning. Then answer the questions below. As you read the selection, notice how each vocabulary word is used.

terrain: piece of land and its natural features

escalated: increased; expanded

tempest: severe storm

rife: filled; widespread

pulsate: vibrate; quiver

intermittently: off and on

inertia: unwillingness to move or act

recoiled: cringed at a repulsive occurrence

appalling: frightful; horrifying

retrieve: recover; get back

1. Which word describes what you do if you drop your glasses in a pool and then jump in and pick them up?

2. Which word could name a thunderstorm with high winds and severe lightning?

3. Which word might be used in talking about a hilly area with small pine trees and a rocky soil?

4. Which word might name the condition of a person who sits in front of the television for hours on end?

5. Which word is an antonym for *decreased*?

1   From the Balcony I descended a few hundred feet down a broad, gentle snow gully without incident, but then things began to get sketchy. The route meandered through out-croppings of broken shale[1] blanketed with six inches of fresh snow. Negotiating the puzzling, infirm <u>terrain</u> demanded unceasing concentration, an all-but-impossible feat in my punch-drunk state.

2   Because the wind had erased the tracks of the climbers who'd gone down before me, I had difficulty determining the correct route.… Fighting to maintain a grip on reality, I started talking to myself out loud. "Keep it together, keep it together, keep it together," I chanted over and over, mantra-like. "You can't afford to [louse] things up here. This is way serious. Keep it together."

3   I sat down to rest on a broad, sloping ledge, but after a few minutes a deafening BOOM! frightened me back to my feet. Enough new snow had accumulated that I feared a massive slab avalanche had released on the slopes above, but when I spun around to look I saw nothing. Then there was another boom!, accompanied by a flash that momentarily lit up the sky, and I realized I was hearing the crash of thunder.

4   In the morning, on the way up, I'd made a point of continually studying the route on this part of the mountain, frequently looking down to pick out landmarks that would be helpful on the descent, compulsively memorizing the terrain: "Remember to turn left at the buttress that looks like a ship's prow. Then follow that skinny line of snow until it curves sharply to the right." This was something I'd trained myself to do many years earlier, a drill I forced myself to go through every time I climbed, and on Everest it may have saved my life. By 6:00 P.M., as the storm <u>escalated</u> into a full-scale blizzard with driving snow and winds gusting in excess of 60 knots, I came upon the rope that had been fixed by the Montenegrins on the snow slope 600 feet above the Col. Sobered by the force of the rising <u>tempest</u>, I realized that I'd gotten down the trickiest ground just in the nick of time.

5   Wrapping the fixed line around my arms to rappel,[2] I continued down through the blizzard. Some minutes later I was overwhelmed by a disturbingly familiar feeling of suffocation, and I realized that my oxygen had once again run out. Three hours earlier when I'd attached my regulator to my third and last oxygen canister, I'd noticed that the gauge indicated that the bottle was only half full. I'd figured that would be enough to get me most of the way down, though, so I hadn't bothered exchanging it for a full one. And now the gas was gone.

6   I pulled the mask from my face, left it hanging around my neck, and pressed onward, surprisingly unconcerned. However, without supplemental oxygen, I moved more slowly, and I had to stop and rest more often.

7   The literature of Everest is <u>rife</u> with accounts of hallucinatory experiences attributable to hypoxia[3] and fatigue. In 1933, the noted English climber Frank Smythe observed "two curious looking objects floating in the sky" directly above him at 27,000 feet: "[One] possessed what appeared to be squat underdeveloped wings, and the other a protuberance suggestive of a beak. They hovered motionless but seemed slowly to <u>pulsate</u>." In 1980, during his solo ascent, Reinhold Messner imagined that an invisible companion was climbing beside him. Gradually, I became aware that my mind had gone haywire in a similar fashion, and I observed my own slide from reality with a blend of fascination and horror.

8   I was so far beyond ordinary exhaustion that I experienced a queer detachment from my body, as if I were observing my descent from a few feet overhead. I imagined that I was dressed in a green cardigan and wingtips. And although the gale was generating a windchill in excess of seventy below zero Fahrenheit, I felt strangely, disturbingly warm.

9   At 6:30, as the last of the daylight seeped from the sky, I'd descended to within 200 vertical feet of Camp Four. Only one obstacle now stood between me and safety: a bulging incline of hard, glassy ice that I would have to descend without a rope. Snow pellets borne by 70-knot gusts stung my face; any exposed flesh was instantly frozen. The tents, no more than 650 horizontal feet away, were only <u>intermittently</u> visible through the whiteout. There was no margin for error. Worried about making a critical blunder, I sat down to marshal my energy before descending further.

10   Once I was off my feet, <u>inertia</u> took hold. It was so much easier to remain at rest than to summon the initiative to tackle the dangerous ice slope; so I

---

[1]*shale:* rock made of hardened clay that splits easily
[2]*rappel:* lower oneself down from a cliff with a rope tied around one's body

[3]*hypoxia:* condition of not enough oxygen in the blood

just sat there as the storm roared around me, letting my mind drift, doing nothing for perhaps forty-five minutes.

11   I'd tightened the draw-strings on my hood until only a tiny opening remained around my eyes, and I was removing the useless, frozen oxygen mask from beneath my chin when Andy Harris suddenly appeared out of the gloom beside me. Shining my headlamp in his direction, I reflexively <u>recoiled</u> when I saw the <u>appalling</u> condition of his face. His cheeks were coated with an armor of frost, one eye was frozen shut, and he was slurring his words badly. He looked in serious trouble. "Which way to the tents?" Andy blurted, frantic to reach shelter.

12   I pointed in the direction of Camp Four, then warned him about the ice just below us. "It's steeper than it looks!" I yelled, straining to make myself heard over the tempest. "Maybe I should go down first and get a rope from camp—" As I was in midsentence, Andy abruptly turned away and moved over the lip of the ice slope, leaving me sitting there dumbfounded.

13   Scooting on his butt, he started down the steepest part of the incline. "Andy," I shouted after him, "it's crazy to try it like that! You're going to blow it for sure!" He yelled something back, but his words were carried off by the screaming wind. A second later he lost his purchase, flipped ass over teakettle, and was suddenly rocketing headfirst down the ice.

14   Two hundred feet below, I could just make out Andy's motionless form slumped at the foot of the incline. I was sure he'd broken at least a leg, maybe his neck. But then, incredibly, he stood up, waved that he was O.K., and started lurching toward Camp Four, which, at the moment was in plain sight, 500 feet beyond.

15   I could see the shadowy forms of three or four people standing outside the tents; their headlamps flickered through curtains of blowing snow. I

"In the morning, on the way up, I'd made a point of continually studying the route on this part of the mountain, frequently looking down to pick out landmarks that would be helpful on the descent."

watched Harris walk toward them across the flats, a distance he covered in less than ten minutes. When the clouds closed in a moment later, cutting off my view, he was within sixty feet of the tents, maybe closer. I didn't see him again after that, but I was certain that he'd reached the security of camp, where Chuldum and Arita would doubtless be waiting with hot tea. Sitting out in the storm, with the ice bulge still standing between me and the tents, I felt a pang of envy. I was angry that my guide hadn't waited for me.

16   My backpack held little more than three empty oxygen canisters and a pint of frozen lemonade; it probably weighed no more than sixteen or eighteen pounds. But I was tired, and worried about getting down the incline without pack over the edge and hoped it would come to rest where I could <u>retrieve</u> it. Then I stood up and started down the ice, which was as smooth and hard as the surface of a bowling ball.

17   Fifteen minutes of dicey, fatiguing crampon[4] work brought me safely to the bottom of the incline, where I easily located my pack, and another ten minutes after that I was in camp myself. I lunged into my tent with my crampons still on, zipped the door tight, and sprawled across the frost-covered floor too tired to even sit upright. For the first time I had a sense of how wasted I really was: I was more exhausted than I'd ever been in my life. But I was safe. Andy was safe. The others would be coming into camp soon. We'd done it. We'd climbed Everest. It had been a little sketchy there for a while, but in the end everything had turned out great.

18   It would be many hours before I learned that everything had not in fact turned out great—that nineteen men and women were stranded up on the mountain by the storm, caught in a desperate struggle for their lives.

---

[4]*crampon:* spiked plate on a shoe to prevent slipping

Starting Time	
Finishing Time	
Reading Time	
Reading Rate	

COMPREHENSION

Read the following questions and statements. For each one, put an X in the box before the option that contains the most complete or accurate answer.

1. The author's destination on this part of his descent was
   - ☐ a. the Balcony.
   - ☐ b. Camp Four.
   - ☐ c. the bottom of the mountain.
   - ☐ d. Camp Two.

2. Climbers carry oxygen
   - ☐ a. so that they can convert it into water if necessary.
   - ☐ b. for protection in a blizzard.
   - ☐ c. to make it easier to breathe in the high altitudes.
   - ☐ d. to leave along the route for other climbers having trouble.

3. This selection is presented
   - ☐ a. in time order.
   - ☐ b. in spatial order.
   - ☐ c. in order of importance.
   - ☐ d. with alternating explanations and examples.

4. The descent was made difficult by
   - ☐ a. the fact that the author was alone.
   - ☐ b. the storm.
   - ☐ c. his mental confusion.
   - ☐ d. both the storm and his mental confusion.

5. The author describes other climbers' hallucinations in order to
   - ☐ a. make the story more interesting.
   - ☐ b. show that even experienced climbers can get confused.
   - ☐ c. prove that many climbers are daredevils.
   - ☐ d. show how different his hallucination was from that of the others.

6. The author sat unmoving in the snow for forty-five minutes because
   - ☐ a. the lack of oxygen was making him a little crazy.
   - ☐ b. he was waiting for his friend Andy.
   - ☐ c. he knew it was important to descend slowly.
   - ☐ d. he was close enough to the tents that he didn't have to worry.

7. The final paragraph of the selection suggests that
   - ☐ a. the author will soon have to climb back up the mountain.
   - ☐ b. stormy weather usually causes hallucinations.
   - ☐ c. people should never climb alone.
   - ☐ d. some of the climbers will not make it down.

8. In paragraphs 12 and 13, the author's tone becomes
   - ☐ a. joyful.
   - ☐ b. worried.
   - ☐ c. unconcerned.
   - ☐ d. angry.

9. Climbing a mountain like Everest requires a person to
   - ☐ a. have no fear.
   - ☐ b. have an ability to carry heavy weights.
   - ☐ c. be physically and mentally prepared.
   - ☐ d. get along well with his or her companions.

10. The expression "curtains of blowing snow" in paragraph 15 is
    - ☐ a. a simile.
    - ☐ b. a metaphor.
    - ☐ c. onomatopoeia.
    - ☐ d. a literal description.

Comprehension Skills Key

1. recalling specific facts	6. making a judgment
2. retaining concepts	7. making an inference
3. organizing facts	8. recognizing tone
4. understanding the main idea	9. understanding characters
5. drawing a conclusion	10. appreciating literary forms

VOCABULARY—PART TWO

Write the word that makes the most sense in each sentence.

escalated   **tempest**
intermittently   **recoiled**
retrieve

1. The climber had seen severe storms before, but this one was truly a _____ .

2. When he bent over to _____ his lost glove, the wind almost blew him away.

3. For a while the storm lessened in intensity, but then suddenly it _____ .

4. Now he could barely see the searchlight blinking _____ in the distance.

5. Even the dogs _____ from going out in the seventy-mile-an-hour winds.

inertia   **rife**
pulsate   **terrain**
appalling

6. The literature of mountain climbing is _____ with stories of disasters.

7. The tricky _____ often causes climbers to lose their footing.

8. _____ weather conditions at very high altitudes can frighten the strongest of climbers.

9. Some find their hearts beating so fast that they can feel them _____ within their bodies.

10. Others slow down almost to the point of _____ .

Comprehension   [ ]

Vocabulary   [ ]

UNDERSTANDING THROUGH WRITING

The author last saw Andy when Andy was sixty feet from the tents. Do you think Andy made it back safely? Write an explanation of what you think. Use specifics from the story to support your answer.

_____
_____
_____
_____
_____
_____
_____
_____
_____
_____
_____
_____

BUILDING STUDY SKILLS

Read the following passage and answer the questions that follow it.

Comprehension and Reading, I

Reading is both a visual and a mental skill. The visual parts involve seeing the words; the mental parts involve understanding them. So the first skills needed for thorough comprehension are word recognition skills.

Depending on what the words are, we recognize them by remembering them, pronouncing them, or analyzing them. Words that we remember are the ones in our sight vocabularies. These are the words we see often enough to recognize on sight. Good readers—sight readers—have developed a large vocabulary of words that they recognize at once while reading. Frequently in reading clinics and reading improvement courses, projectors are used to flash sight words on the screen for fractions of a second. That training is designed to enhance and reinforce the reader's stock of sight words.

Sometimes we see words that we do not recognize. Then we slow down to sound out or pronounce them. Many of these words are in our listening vocabulary—that is, they are words we know when they are spoken aloud. Our knowledge of phonics helps us to pronounce unfamiliar words and move words from our listening vocabulary into our sight vocabulary.

If we do not recognize a word even after we have sounded it out, then we need to analyze it. Analyzing a word means breaking it down in recognizable pieces. Our knowledge of syllabication and word parts helps us to do this.

To become competent readers, we need to use all three of the word recognition skills.

1. The words that we remember are the words in our _____ vocabularies.

2. If you saw the word *hallucination* in Jon Krakauer's story and were not sure that you recognized it, the first thing you would do would be to try to _____ it.

3. Our knowledge of _____ helps us to pronounce unfamiliar words.

4. Analyzing a word means breaking it down into _____ pieces.

5. If you did not know the word *disturbingly* in Krakauer's story even after you had pronounced it, you might be able to figure out the meaning by _____ its parts.

A Match to the Heart

Gretel Ehrlich

READING PURPOSE—
In this selection a woman is struck by lightning. As you read, look for passages that describe her physical condition.

VOCABULARY—PART ONE

All of these words are in the selection you are about to read. Study each word and its meaning. Then answer the questions below. As you read the selection, notice how each vocabulary word is used.

elapsed: gone by

erratically: in an irregular way

bleakness: cheerless, depressing situation

scavengers: animals that prey on dead bodies

incoherently: not making any sense

gurney: cart for moving patients in a hospital

aura: a quality or atmosphere given off by a person

transition: a changing from one condition to another

fortuitous: fortunate; lucky

lacerations: cuts; wounds

1. Which word names something you might find in an emergency room?

2. Which word could describe how you felt if you found a hundred-dollar bill on the street?

3. Which word describes what the victims of an auto accident might have on their bodies?

4. Which word might describe birds such as vultures?

5. Which word might someone use in identifying the age of twenty-one, when a person can drink alcoholic beverages legally?

1   Before electricity carved its blue path toward me, before the negative charge shot down from cloud to ground, before "streamers" jumped the positive charge back up from ground to cloud, before air expanded and contracted producing loud pressure pulses I could not hear because I was already dead, I had been walking.

2   When I started out on foot that August afternoon, the thunderstorm was blowing in fast. On the face of the mountain, a mile ahead, hard westerly gusts and sudden updrafts collided, pulling black clouds apart. Yet the storm looked harmless. When a distant thunderclap scared the dogs, I called them to my side and rubbed their ears: "Don't worry, you're okay as long as you're with me."

3   I woke in a pool of blood, lying on my stomach some distance from where I should have been, flung at an odd angle to one side of the dirt path. The whole sky had grown dark. Was it evening, and if so, which one? How many minutes or hours had <u>elapsed</u> since I lost consciousness, and where were the dogs? I tried to call out to them but my voice didn't work. The muscles in my throat were paralyzed and I couldn't swallow. Were the dogs dead? Everything was terribly wrong: I had trouble seeing, talking, breathing, and I couldn't move my legs or right arm. Nothing remained in my memory—no sounds, flashes, smells, no warnings of any kind. Had I been shot in the back? Had I suffered a stroke or heart attack? These thoughts were dark pools in sand.

4   The sky was black. Was this a storm in the middle of the day or was it night with a storm traveling through? When thunder exploded over me, I knew I had been hit by lightning.

5   The pain in my chest intensified and every muscle in my body ached. I was quite sure I was dying....

6   It started to rain. Every time a drop hit bare skin there was an explosion of pain. Blood crusted my left eye. I touched my good hand to my heart, which was beating wildly, <u>erratically</u>. My chest was numb, as if it had been sprayed with novocaine. No feeling of peace filled me. Death was a <u>bleakness,</u> a grayness about which it was impossible to be curious or relieved. I loved those dogs and hoped they weren't badly hurt. If I didn't die soon, how many days would pass before we were found, and when would the <u>scavengers</u> come? The sky was dark, or was that the way life flew out of the body, in a long tube with no light at the end? I lay on the cold ground waiting. The mountain was purple, and sage stirred against my face. I knew I had to give up all this, then my own body and all my thinking. Once more I lifted my head to look for the dogs but, unable to see them, I twisted myself until I faced east and tried to let go of all desire.

7   When my eyes opened again I knew I wasn't dead. Images from World War II movies filled my head: of wounded soldiers dragging themselves across a field, and if I could have laughed—that is, made my face work into a smile and get sounds to discharge from my throat—I would have. God, it would have been good to laugh. Instead, I considered my options: either lie there and wait for someone to find me—how many days or weeks would that take?—or somehow get back to the house. I calmly assessed what might be wrong with me—stroke, cerebral hemorrhage, gunshot wound—but it was bigger than I could understand. The instinct to survive does not rise from particulars; a deep but general misery rollercoasted me into action. I tried to propel myself on my elbows but my right arm didn't work. The wind had swung round and was blowing in from the east. It was still a dry storm with only sputtering rain, but when I raised myself up, lightning fingered the entire sky.

8   It is not true that lightning never strikes the same place twice. I had entered a shower of sparks and furious brightness and, worried that I might be struck again, watched as lightning touched down all around me. Years before, in the high country, I'd been hit by lightning: an electrical charge had rolled down an open meadow during a fearsome thunderstorm, surged up the legs of my horse, coursed through me, and bounced a big spark off the top of my head. To be struck again—and this time it was a direct hit—what did it mean?

9   The feeling had begun to come back into my legs and after many awkward attempts, I stood. To walk meant lifting each leg up by the thigh, moving it forward with my hands, setting it down. The earth felt like a peach that had split open in the middle; one side moved up while the other side moved down and my legs were out of rhythm. The ground rolled the way it does during an earthquake and the sky was tattered book pages waving in different directions. Was the ground liquifying under

me, or had the molecular composition of my body deliquesced?[1] I struggled to piece together fragments. Then it occurred to me that my brain was torn and that's where the blood had come from.

"It was still a dry storm with only sputtering rain, but when I raised myself up, lightning fingered the entire sky."

10   I walked. Sometimes my limbs held me, sometimes they didn't. I don't know how many times I fell but it didn't matter because I was making slow progress toward home.

11   Home—the ranch house—was about a quarter of a mile away. I don't remember much about getting there. My concentration went into making my legs work. The storm was strong. All the way across the basin, lightning lifted parts of mountains and sky into yellow refulgence[2] and dropped them again, only to lift others. The inside of my eyelids turned gold and I could see the dark outlines of things through them. At the bottom of the hill I opened the door to my pickup and blew the horn with the idea that someone might hear me. No one came. My head had swollen to an indelicate shape. I tried to swallow—I was so thirsty—but the muscles in my throat were still paralyzed and I wondered when I would no longer be able to breathe.

12   Inside the house, sounds began to come out of me. I was doing crazy things, ripping my hiking boots off because the bottoms of my feet were burning, picking up the phone when I was finally able to scream. One of those times, someone happened to be on the line. I was screaming incoherently for help. My last conscious act was to dial 911....

13   The ambulance rocked and slid, slamming my bruised body against the metal rails of the gurney. Every muscle was in violent spasm and there was a place on my back near the heart that burned. I heard myself yell in pain. Finally the EMT's rolled up towels and blankets and wedged them against

my arms, shoulders, hips, and knees so the jolting of the vehicle wouldn't dislodge me. The ambulance slid down into ditches, struggled out, bumped from one deep rut to another. I asked to be taken to the hospital in Cody, but they said they were afraid my heart might stop again. As it was, the local hospital was thirty-five miles away, ten of them dirt, and the trip took more than an hour....

14   When the doctor on call—the only doctor in town, waddled into what they called the emergency room, my aura, he said, was yellow and gray—a soul in transition. I knew that he had gone to medical school but had never completed a residency and had been barred from ER or ICU work in the hospitals of Florida, where he had lived previously. Yet I was lucky. Florida has many lightning victims, and unlike the doctors I would see later, he at least recognized the symptoms of a lightning strike. The tally sheet read this way: I had suffered a hit by lightning which caused ventricular fibrillation—cardiac arrest—though luckily my heart started beating again. Violent contractions of muscles when one is hit often cause the body to fly through the air: I was flung far and hit hard on my left side, which may have caused my heart to start again, but along with that fortuitous side effect, I sustained a concussion, broken ribs, a possible broken jaw, and lacerations above the eye. The paralysis below my waist and up through the chest and throat—called kerauno-paralysis—is common in lightning strikes and almost always temporary, but my right arm continued to be almost useless. Fernlike burns—arborescent erythema—covered my entire body. These occur when the electrical charge follows tracings of moisture on the skin—rain or sweat—thus the spidery red lines....

15   The nurses loaded me onto a gurney. As they wheeled me down the hall to my room, a front

_____

[1]*deliquesced:* dissolved; became liquid
[2]*refulgence:* radiance; brightness

wheel fell off and I was slammed into the wall. Once I was in bed, the deep muscle aches continued, as did the chest pains. Later, friends came to visit. Neither doctor nor nurse had cleaned the cuts on my head, so Laura, who had herded sheep and cowboyed on all the ranches where I had lived and whose wounds I had cleaned when my saddle horse dragged her across a high mountain pasture, wiped blood and dirt from my face, arms, and hands with a cool towel and spooned yogurt into my mouth.

16   I was the only patient in the hospital. During the night, sheet lightning inlaid the walls with cool gold. I felt like an ancient, mummified child who had been found on a rock ledge near our ranch: bound tightly, unable to move, my dead face tipped backwards toward the moon....

Starting Time	
Finishing Time	
Reading Time	
Reading Rate	

COMPREHENSION

Read the following questions and statements. For each one, put an X in the box before the option that contains the most complete or accurate answer.

1. The events in this story take place in
   - ☐ a. August.
   - ☐ b. October.
   - ☐ c. January.
   - ☐ d. April.

2. The author
   - ☐ a. knows several people who have been struck by lightning.
   - ☐ b. has been struck twice herself.
   - ☐ c. is struck for the first time in this story.
   - ☐ d. is struck for the first time in this story, as are her dogs.

3. In paragraph 7, the writer focuses mostly on
   - ☐ a. a description of where she was when the lightning hit her.
   - ☐ b. a history of famous lightning strikes.
   - ☐ c. a description of the physical sensations she experienced.
   - ☐ d. a narrative of how she walked to her house.

4. The general purpose of this selection is to tell about
   - ☐ a. the author's courage.
   - ☐ b. how her body feels and how she tries to get help after being struck by lightning.
   - ☐ c. how worried she was about her dogs.
   - ☐ d. people's universal fear of lightning.

5. The hospital where the author goes for treatment
   - ☐ a. is well-known for treating lightning victims.
   - ☐ b. is situated in a large city about fifty miles away.
   - ☐ c. is overcrowded with other accident victims.
   - ☐ d. gives sloppy, barely competent care.

6. The author's situation was made more difficult by
   - ☐ a. her stubbornness.
   - ☐ b. her isolation.
   - ☐ c. her fear.
   - ☐ d. the intensity of the storm.

7. The author probably survived the lightning strike because
   - ☐ a. it was not a direct hit.
   - ☐ b. landing hard on the ground started her heart pumping again.
   - ☐ c. an earlier hit had made her immune to the worst dangers.
   - ☐ d. she got to the hospital right away.

8. The tone the author uses in paragraph 3 is one of
   - ☐ a. bewilderment.
   - ☐ b. anger.
   - ☐ c. sadness.
   - ☐ d. confidence.

9. The doctor that the author sees
   - ☐ a. is a fairly famous heart surgeon.
   - ☐ b. was probably a good choice in this particular situation.
   - ☐ c. had never worked in Florida, where lightning strikes are common.
   - ☐ d. ignores her for several hours.

10. When the author says that "lightning fingered the entire sky," she is using
    ☐ a. alliteration.
    ☐ b. a simile.
    ☐ c. a metaphor.
    ☐ d. a literal description.

Comprehension Skills Key

1. recalling specific facts
2. retaining concepts
3. organizing facts
4. understanding the main idea
5. drawing a conclusion
6. making a judgment
7. making an inference
8. recognizing tone
9. understanding characters
10. appreciating literary forms

VOCABULARY—PART TWO

Write the word that makes the most sense in each sentence.

elapsed	bleakness
scavengers	transition
lacerations	

1. Lying waiting to die, the author wondered when _____ would come looking for her body.

2. Blood was pouring out of the _____ on her face and arms.

3. A feeling of _____ and despair overtook her.

4. Though only minutes had passed, it seemed like hours had _____ .

5. She felt that her soul was in _____ from this life to the next.

aura	fortuitous
erratically	incoherently
gurney	

6. It was _____ that the author was finally able to call for help; otherwise, she certainly would have died.

7. Even though she was babbling _____ on the telephone, the operator was able to understand her.

8. She was able to explain that instead of beating regularly, her heart was jumping _____ .

9. She was wheeled into the hospital on a(n) _____ .

10. A(n) _____ of death seemed to be coming from the top of her head.

Comprehension	☐
Vocabulary	☐

UNDERSTANDING THROUGH WRITING

Write a description of the place where the lightning strike occurred. Use details from the selection to make your description come alive.

_____

_____

_____

_____

_____

_____

_____

_____

BUILDING STUDY SKILLS

Read the following passage and answer the questions that follow it.

Comprehension and Reading, II

Other aspects of reading comprehension follow word recognition. These include retention, organization, interpretation, and appreciation.

In retention, the reader is called upon to isolate details, to recall specifics, and to retain concepts. All of these skills are applied to remembering facts that have been read.

The reader is also expected to organize as he or she reads. Ways to organize are as follows:

1. Classifying. A good reader will arrange facts in groups while reading. In that way, facts that contribute to comprehension of a concept are seen as a unit, separate from those that deal with other concepts.

2. Establishing a Sequence. For true understanding of the author's ideas, the reader must be aware of the order in which events take place. It is easier to understand a fact when it is seen as part of a related whole. Think of each new fact as adding to the previous one and laying a foundation for the next.

3. Following Directions. Too many readers fail to follow directions, despite the important part they play in comprehension. Following directions is an organizing skill that requires the reader to arrange facts and to understand the steps he or she must follow. Readers often do not heed directions because they are unable to classify facts properly, or they are unable to establish a correct sequence.

4. Seeing Relationships. An author puts forth ideas in an organized fashion, presenting first the concepts needed to understand other, more-complex concepts that follow. The reader must grasp the relationship between these concepts for true comprehension.

5. Generalizing. This skill requires the reader to arrive at general rules or theories derived from the specific facts that the author has presented.

1. The comprehension skill that enables the reader to recall specifics is called _____ .

2. For example, when you read Ehrlich's story you should have remembered that the season the strike occurred in was _____ .

3. Classifying is one way a reader can _____ facts.

4. To establish a sequence, the reader must be aware of the _____ in which events take place.

5. In Ehrlich's story, you must be aware that before she tried to save herself, her first reaction was that she was going to _____ .

Alive

Piers Paul Read

READING PURPOSE—
This selection explains the dilemma of the survivors of an airplane crash who have gone without food for ten days. Read to learn how they solve their problem.

VOCABULARY—PART ONE

All of these words are in the selection you are about to read. Study each word and its meaning. Then answer the questions below. As you read the selection, notice how each vocabulary word is used.

modest: limited

strident: harsh; grating

sustenance: nourishment

repugnant: offensive; disgusting

lucid: clearly understood

expediency: desirability or fitness under the circumstances

incontestable: unarguable; certain

allayed: calmed; relieved

prevailed: took control; won out

irrational: unreasonable; not sensible

1. Which word could describe an explanation so clear that it makes perfect sense to everyone in a class?

   _____

2. Which word could be a synonym for *food*?

   _____

3. Which word describes a fear that you can't get over even though you know there is no reason for it?

   _____

4. Which word might describe evidence so strong that it will absolutely convince a jury?

   _____

5. Which word might describe the act of blowing one's nose in one's hand?

   _____

1   They awoke on the morning of Sunday, October 22, to face their tenth day on the mountain. First to leave the plane were Marcelo Pérez and Roy Harley. Roy had found a transistor radio between two seats and by using a <u>modest</u> knowledge of electronics, acquired when helping a friend construct a hi-fi system, he had been able to make it work. It was difficult to receive signals in the deep cleft between the huge mountains, so Roy made an aerial with strands of wire from the plane's electric circuits. While he turned the dial, Marcelo held the aerial and moved it around. They picked up scraps of broadcasts from Chile but no news of the rescue effort. All that came over the radio waves were the <u>strident</u> voices of Chilean politicians embroiled in the strike by the middle classes against the socialist government of President Allende.

2   Few of the other boys came out into the snow. Starvation was taking its effect. They were becoming weaker and more listless. When they stood up they felt faint and found it difficult to keep their balance. They felt cold, even when the sun rose to warm them, and their skin started to grow wrinkled like that of old men.

3   Their food supplies were running out. The daily ration of a scrap of chocolate, a capful of wine, and a teaspoonful of jam or canned fish—eaten slowly to make it last—was more torture than <u>sustenance</u> for these healthy, athletic boys; yet the strong shared it with the weak, the healthy with the injured. It was clear to them all that they could not survive much longer. It was not so much that they were consumed with ravenous hunger as that they felt themselves grow weaker each day, and no knowledge of medicine or nutrition was required to predict how it would end.

4   Their minds turned to other sources of food. It seemed impossible that there should be nothing whatsoever growing in the Andes, for even the meanest form of plant life might provide some nutrition. In the immediate vicinity of the plane there was only snow. The nearest soil was a hundred feet beneath them. The only ground exposed to sun and air was barren mountain rock on which they found nothing but brittle lichens. They scraped some of it off and mixed it into a paste with melted snow, but the taste was bitter and disgusting, and as food it was worthless. Except for lichens there was nothing. Some thought of the cushions, but even these were not stuffed with straw. Nylon and foam rubber would not help them.

5   For some days several of the boys had realized that if they were to survive they would have to eat the bodies of those who had died in the crash. It was a ghastly prospect. The corpses lay around the plane in the snow, preserved by the intense cold in the state in which they had died. While the thought of cutting flesh from those who had been their friends was deeply <u>repugnant</u> to them all, a <u>lucid</u> appreciation of their predicament led them to consider it.

6   Gradually the discussion spread as these boys cautiously mentioned it to their friends or to those they thought would be sympathetic. Finally, Canessa brought it out into the open. He argued forcefully that they were not going to be rescued; that they would have to escape themselves, but that nothing could be done without food; and that the only food was human flesh. He used his knowledge of medicine to describe, in his penetrating, high-pitched voice, how their bodies were using up their reserves. "Every time you move," he said, "you use up part of your own body. Soon we shall be so weak that we won't have the strength even to cut the meat that is lying there before our eyes."

7   Canessa did not argue just from <u>expediency</u>. He insisted that they had a moral duty to stay alive by any means at their disposal, and because Canessa was earnest about his religious belief, great weight was given to what he said by the more pious among the survivors.

8   "It is meat," he said. "That's all it is. The souls have left their bodies and are in heaven with God. All that is left here are the carcasses, which are no more human beings than the dead flesh of the cattle we eat at home."…

9   The truth of what he said was <u>incontestable</u>.

10   A meeting was called inside the Fairchild, and for the first time all twenty-seven survivors discussed the issue which faced them—whether or not they should eat the bodies of the dead to survive. Canessa, Zerbino, Fernández, and Fito Strauch repeated the arguments they had used before. If they did not they would die. It was their moral obligation to live, for their own sake and for the sake of their families. God wanted them to live, and he had given them the means to do so in the dead bodies of their friends. If God had not wished them to live, they would have been killed in the accident; it would be wrong now to reject this gift of life because they were too squeamish.

11   "But what have we done," asked Marcelo, "that God now asks us to eat the bodies of our dead friends?"

12 There was a moment's hesitation. Then Zerbino turned to his captain and said, "But what do you think *they* would have thought?"

13 Marcelo did not answer.

14 "I know," Zerbino went on, "that if my dead body could help you to stay alive, then I'd certainly want you to use it. In fact, if I do die and you don't eat me, then I'll come back from wherever I am and give you a good kick in the ass."

15 This argument <u>allayed</u> many doubts, for however reluctant each boy might be to eat the flesh of a friend, all of them agreed with Zerbino. There and then they made a pact that if any more of them were to die, their bodies were to be used as food.

16 Marcelo still shrank from a decision. He and his diminishing party of optimists held on to the hope of rescue, but few of the others any longer shared their faith. Indeed, a few of the younger boys went over to the pessimists—or the realists, as they considered themselves—with some resentment against Marcelo Pérez and Pancho Delgado. They felt they had been deceived. The rescue they had been promised had not come.

17 The latter were not without support, however. Coche Inciarte and Numa Turcatti, both strong, tough boys with an inner gentleness, told their companions that while they did not think it would be wrong, they knew that they themselves could not do it. Liliana Methol agreed with them. Her manner was calm as always but, like the others, she grappled with the emotions the issue aroused. Her instinct to survive was strong, her longing for her children was acute, but the thought of eating human flesh horrified her. She did not think it was wrong; she could distinguish between sin and physical revulsion, and a social taboo was not a law of God. "But," she said, "as long as there is a chance of rescue, as long as there is *something* left to eat, even if it is only a morsel of chocolate, then I can't do it."

"Their minds turned to other sources of food.... The only ground exposed to the sun and air was barren mountain rock."

18 Javier Methol agreed with his wife but would not deter others from doing what they felt must be done. No one suggested that God might want them to choose to die. They all believed that virtue lay in survival and that eating their dead friends would in no way endanger their souls, but it was one thing to decide and another to act.

19 Their discussions had continued most of the day, and by midafternoon they knew that they must act now or not at all, yet they sat inside the plane in total silence. At last a group of four—Canessa, Maspons, Zerbino, and Fito Strauch—rose and went out into the snow. Few followed them. No one wished to know who was going to cut the meat or from which body it was to be taken.

20 Most of the bodies were covered by snow, but the buttocks of one protruded a few yards from the plane. With no exchange of words Canessa knelt, bared the skin, and cut into the flesh with a piece of broken glass. It was frozen hard and difficult to cut, but he persisted until he had cut away twenty slivers the size of matchsticks. He then stood up, went back to the plane, and placed them on the roof.

21 Inside there was silence. The boys cowered in the Fairchild. Canessa told them that the meat was there on the roof, drying in the sun, and that those who wished to do so should come out and eat it. No one came, and again Canessa took it upon himself to prove his resolution. He prayed to God to help him do what he knew to be right and then took a piece of meat in his hand. He hesitated. Even with his mind so firmly made up, the horror of the act paralyzed him. His hand would neither rise to his mouth nor fall to his side while the revulsion which possessed him struggled with his stubborn will. The will <u>prevailed</u>. The hand rose and pushed the meat into his mouth. He swallowed it.

22 He felt triumphant. His conscience had overcome a primitive, <u>irrational</u> taboo. He was going to survive.

23 Later that evening, small groups of boys came out of the plane to follow his example. Zerbino took a strip and swallowed it as Canessa had done, but it stuck in his throat. He scooped a handful of snow into his mouth and managed to wash it down. Fito Strauch followed his example, then Maspons and Vizintin and others.

24 Meanwhile Gustavo Nicolich, the tall, curly-haired boy, only twenty years old, who had done so much to keep up the morale of his young friends, wrote to his *novia* in Montevideo.

Most dear Rosina:

25 I am writing to you from inside the plane (our *petit hotel* for the moment). It is sunset and has started to be rather cold and windy which it usually does at this hour of the evening. Today the weather was wonderful—a beautiful sun and very hot. It reminded me of the days on the beach with you—the big difference being that then we would be going to have lunch at your place at midday whereas now I'm stuck outside the plane without any food at all.

26 Today, on top of everything else, it was rather depressing and a lot of the others began to get discouraged (today is the tenth day we have been here), but luckily this gloom did not spread to me because I get incredible strength just by thinking that I'm going to see you again. Another of the things leading to the general depression is that in a while the food will run out: we have only got two cans of seafood (small), one bottle of white wine, and a little cherry brandy left, which for twenty-six men (well, there are also boys who want to be men) is nothing.

27 One thing which will seem incredible to you —it seems unbelievable to me—is that today we started to cut up the dead in order to eat them. There is nothing else to do. I prayed to God from the bottom of my heart that this day would never come, but it has and we have to face it with courage and faith. Faith, because I came to the conclusion that the bodies are there because God put them there and, since the only thing that matters is the soul, I don't have to feel great remorse; and if the day came and I could save someone with my body, I would gladly do it.

28 I don't know how you, Mama, Papa, or the children can be feeling; you don't know how sad it makes me to think that you are suffering, and I constantly ask God to reassure you and

give us courage because that is the only way of getting out of this. I think that soon there will be a happy ending for everyone.

29 You'll get a shock when you see me. I am dirty, with a beard, and a little thinner, with a big gash on my head, another one on my chest which has healed now, and one very small cut which I got today working in the cabin of the plane, besides various small cuts in the legs and on the shoulder; but in spite of it all, I'm all right.

Starting Time	
Finishing Time	
Reading Time	
Reading Rate	

COMPREHENSION

Read the following questions and statements. For each one, put an X in the box before the option that contains the most complete or accurate answer.

1. The mountains where the plane had crashed were
   ☐ a. the Appalachians.
   ☐ b. the Andes.
   ☐ c. the Rockies.
   ☐ d. the Alps.

2. Liliana Methol could not bring herself to eat the bodies of the dead because she
   ☐ a. could not disregard a social taboo.
   ☐ b. was horrified by the thought of eating human flesh.
   ☐ c. would not disobey God's law.
   ☐ d. had lost interest in living.

3. The boys decided to eat the flesh of their dead friends
   ☐ a. as soon as they realized the nutritional value of such action.
   ☐ b. only after hopes of a rescue faded.
   ☐ c. after every last bit of their food supply was gone.
   ☐ d. before realizing the consequences of their actions.

4. Another title for this selection could be
   - ☐ a. The Moment of Truth.
   - ☐ b. God's Children.
   - ☐ c. Survival of the Fittest.
   - ☐ d. The Great Unknown.

5. To the survivors, the strident voices of Chilean politicians must have seemed
   - ☐ a. like a ray of hope.
   - ☐ b. to be an answer to their prayers.
   - ☐ c. important and comforting.
   - ☐ d. unrealistic and futile.

6. The process by which the survivors decided to eat human flesh to save themselves was
   - ☐ a. extremely difficult.
   - ☐ b. quite ridiculous.
   - ☐ c. totally pointless.
   - ☐ d. completely deceptive.

7. In a warmer climate, the dead bodies would have
   - ☐ a. started to decompose.
   - ☐ b. seemed more appetizing.
   - ☐ c. been impossible to cut up.
   - ☐ d. provided less nourishment.

8. The author's position concerning the personal decisions each survivor had to make is
   - ☐ a. critical.
   - ☐ b. unknown.
   - ☐ c. sentimental.
   - ☐ d. sympathetic.

9. Canessa was
   - ☐ a. indecisive.
   - ☐ b. irrational.
   - ☐ c. determined.
   - ☐ d. callous.

10. The author tries to make the reader
    - ☐ a. believe that eating human flesh is a natural act.
    - ☐ b. despise the boys who ate their dead friends.
    - ☐ c. understand why the boys acted as they did.
    - ☐ d. realize that survival is more important than moral beliefs.

Comprehension Skills Key

1. recalling specific facts
2. retaining concepts
3. organizing facts
4. understanding the main idea
5. drawing a conclusion
6. making a judgment
7. making an inference
8. recognizing tone
9. understanding characters
10. appreciating literary forms

VOCABULARY—PART TWO

Write the word that makes the most sense in each sentence.

modest	**sustenance**
repugnant	**lucid**
irrational	

1. The survivors were starving; they had been without _____ for several days.

2. They had tried to stretch out what they had for as long as possible, but they had only _____ success at this.

3. One boy's _____ explanation of their next option made sense to them, but they still had trouble accepting it.

4. Instead of thinking clear thoughts, the survivors held _____ fears.

5. To eat human flesh was the most _____ thing any of them had ever considered.

expediency   **incontestable**
prevailed   **strident**
allayed

6. Hearing one of the more religious boys support the idea _____ the survivors' fears.

7. He explained the _____ of eating human flesh in their very dire circumstances.

8. He also emphasized the _____ fact that otherwise they would starve to death.

9. Whereas earlier speakers had been _____ , his voice was soft and gentle.

10. Though they were not at all enthusiastic, this boy's viewpoint finally _____ among the group.

Comprehension [ ]

Vocabulary [ ]

UNDERSTANDING THROUGH WRITING

If you were faced with the choice of eating human flesh or starving to death, what do you think you would have done? Write your answer, and then give reasons for your decision.

_____

_____

_____

_____

_____

_____

_____

BUILDING STUDY SKILLS

Read the following passage and answer the questions that follow it.

Comprehension and Reading, III

As we have seen, retention and organization are two aspects of comprehension. Two other areas are interpretation and appreciation, which are made up of six skills.

1. Understanding the Main Idea. Proper interpretation of material is based on understanding the main idea. Very often, though, the main idea is not stated but must be gathered or interpreted by the reader.

2. Drawing Conclusions. Based on the ideas presented, the reader must make the only judgment or form the only opinion allowed by the facts. There should be no doubt about which conclusion the author expects you to reach.

3. Making Inferences. Unlike a conclusion, an inference is a reasonable judgment based on the facts. The idea you infer may not be the only one suggested. Making inferences is one of the most critical areas of comprehension demanded of the reader.

4. Predicting Outcomes. Authors use ideas to lead the reader to certain ends or objectives. They provide the facts you need to predict the intended result.

5. Making a Judgment. Sometimes the author expects readers to make a judgment suggested by the facts and arguments.

6. Recognizing Tone. Finally, the reader is expected to recognize the author's tone—the joy or sadness of the article. We visualize the reality the author has tried to create, and we see humor—and are moved to laughter—when that has been the goal.

1. Often the main idea of a selection is not directly _____ .

2. In "Alive" the main idea has to do with the survivors' _____ of starving to death.

3. The author lays a groundwork of facts from which the reader can _____ the outcome.

4. Read's description of the situation the survivors were in should have led you to predict that they would finally _____ human flesh.

5. Reacting to the joy, sadness, or even horror of a story is recognizing _____ .

TOPIC REVIEW
React to Topic 4

Respond to one or more of these questions as your instructor directs.

1. The main characters in "The Day I Nearly Drowned," "A Match to the Heart," and "Into Thin Air" have certain things in common as well as certain differences. Choose two of these characters. List three similarities and three differences in their situations.

_____

_____

_____

_____

_____

2. Use the information you developed in question 1 to write about the two characters you chose. Write a paragraph or two describing their similarities and differences.

_____

_____

_____

_____

_____

3. In Building Study Skills 17 you learned how marking the text can be a valuable aid in remembering significant points. Choose a different selection in this topic and mark four or five points that are important to the action in it. When you have finished, go back and summarize each point you marked. These summaries should provide a quick overview of the highlights of the story.

_____

_____

_____

_____

_____

4. Draw a diagram of the setting of either "Alive" or "Into Thin Air." Use information from the selection as much as possible, but make up the parts that are unclear to you. Be sure that your diagram is accurately labeled and includes all of the important elements in the story.

_____

_____

_____

_____

_____

5. Are there certain characteristics people must have to survive great physical challenges? Think about the qualities shown by the characters in this topic or by people you know who have faced similar situations. Write about what you think it takes to overcome intense physical hardship. Give as many specific examples as you can.

_____

_____

_____

_____

_____

6. Pretend that you are a television news announcer assigned to report on the events in either "Autumn Storm" or "A Match to the Heart." Your story will cover three areas: the person involved, the setting, and what actually happened. Write about how you will handle each area. For the person, you should write two or three interview questions. For the setting, you should write what you would show and what you could say about it. For what actually happened, you could summarize the events in a few sentences. Present your newscast in the order that makes the most sense to you.

_____

_____

_____

_____

_____

Words-per-Minute Table

Selection / # words	1	2	3	4	5	6	7	8	9	10	11	12	13	14	15	16	17	18	19	20
# words	1295	1568	1290	1509	1578	1332	1112	1099	1691	1231	2097	1326	1485	1943	1263	2016	1323	1477	1683	2147
1:20	971	1176	968	1132	1184	999	834	824	1268	923	1573	995	1114	1457	947	1512	992	1108	1262	1610
1:40	777	941	774	905	947	799	667	659	1015	739	1258	796	891	1166	758	1210	794	886	1010	1288
2:00	648	784	645	755	789	666	556	550	846	616	1049	663	743	972	632	1008	662	739	842	1074
2:20	555	672	553	647	676	571	477	471	725	528	899	568	636	833	541	864	567	633	721	920
2:40	486	588	484	566	592	500	417	412	634	462	786	497	557	729	474	756	496	554	631	805
3:00	432	523	430	503	526	444	371	366	564	410	699	442	495	648	421	672	441	492	561	716
3:20	389	470	387	453	473	400	334	330	507	369	629	398	446	583	379	605	397	443	505	644
3:40	353	428	352	412	430	363	303	300	461	336	572	362	405	530	344	550	361	403	459	586
4:00	324	392	323	377	395	333	278	275	423	308	524	332	371	486	316	504	331	369	421	537
4:20	299	362	298	348	364	307	257	254	390	284	484	306	343	448	291	465	305	341	388	495
4:40	278	336	276	323	338	285	238	236	362	264	449	284	318	416	271	432	284	317	361	460
5:00	259	314	258	302	316	266	222	220	338	246	419	265	297	389	253	403	265	295	337	429
5:20	243	294	242	283	296	250	209	206	317	231	393	249	278	364	237	378	248	277	316	403
5:40	229	277	228	266	278	235	196	194	298	217	370	234	262	343	223	356	233	261	297	379
6:00	216	261	215	252	263	222	185	183	282	205	350	221	248	324	211	336	221	246	281	358
6:20	204	248	204	238	249	210	176	174	267	194	331	209	234	307	199	318	209	233	266	339
6:40	194	235	194	226	237	200	167	165	254	185	315	199	223	291	189	302	198	222	252	322
7:00	185	224	184	216	225	190	159	157	242	176	300	189	212	278	180	288	189	211	240	307
7:20	177	214	176	206	215	182	152	150	231	168	286	181	203	265	172	275	180	201	230	293
7:40	169	205	168	197	206	174	145	143	221	161	274	173	194	253	165	263	173	193	220	280
8:00	162	196	161	189	197	167	139	137	211	154	262	166	186	243	158	252	165	185	210	268
8:20	155	188	155	181	189	160	133	132	203	148	252	159	178	233	152	242	159	177	202	258
8:40	149	181	149	174	182	154	128	127	195	142	242	153	171	224	146	233	153	170	194	248
9:00	144	174	143	168	175	148	124	122	188	137	233	147	165	216	140	224	147	164	187	239
9:20	139	168	138	162	169	143	119	118	181	132	225	142	159	208	135	216	142	158	180	230
9:40	134	162	133	156	163	138	115	114	175	127	217	137	154	201	131	209	137	153	174	222
10:00	130	157	129	151	158	133	111	110	169	123	210	133	149	194	126	202	132	148	168	215
10:20	125	152	125	146	153	129	108	106	164	119	203	128	144	188	122	195	128	143	163	208
10:40	121	147	121	141	148	125	104	103	159	115	197	124	139	182	118	189	124	138	158	201
11:00	118	143	117	137	143	121	101	100	154	112	191	121	135	177	115	183	120	134	153	195
11:20	114	138	114	133	139	118	98	97	149	109	185	117	131	171	111	178	117	130	149	189
11:40	111	134	111	129	135	114	95	94	145	106	180	114	127	167	108	173	113	127	144	184
12:00	108	131	108	126	132	111	93	92	141	103	175	111	124	162	105	168	110	123	140	179
12:20	105	127	105	122	128	108	90	89	137	100	170	108	120	158	102	163	107	120	136	174
12:40	102	124	102	119	125	105	88	87	134	97	166	105	117	153	100	159	104	117	133	170
13:00	100	121	99	116	121	102	86	85	130	95	161	102	114	149	97	155	102	114	129	165
13:20	97	118	97	113	118	100	83	82	127	92	157	99	111	146	95	151	99	111	126	161
13:40	95	115	94	110	115	97	81	80	124	90	153	97	109	142	92	148	97	108	123	157
14:00	93	112	92	108	113	95	79	79	121	88	150	95	106	139	90	144	95	106	120	153
14:20	90	109	90	105	110	93	78	77	118	86	146	93	104	136	88	141	92	103	117	150
14:40	88	107	88	103	108	91	76	75	115	84	143	90	101	132	86	137	90	101	115	146
15:00	86	105	86	101	105	89	74	73	113	82	140	88	99	130	84	134	88	98	112	143

Minutes and Seconds Elapsed

136

Progress Graph

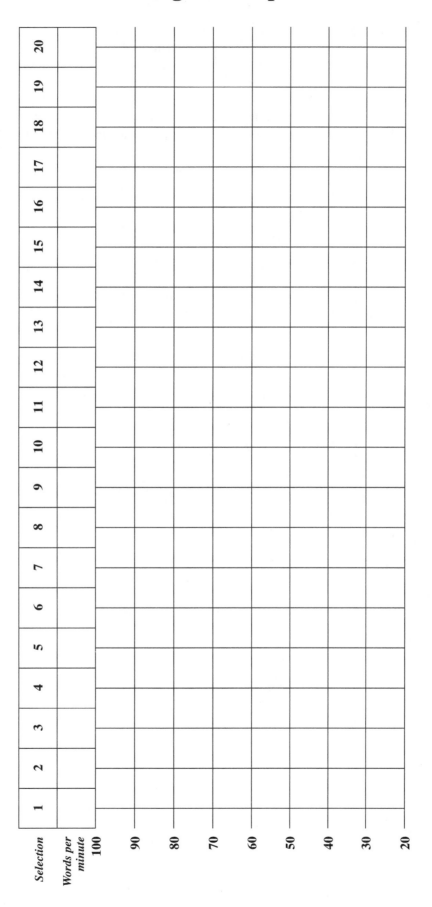

Comprehension Skills Profile

The graph below is designed to help you see your areas of comprehension weakness. Because all the comprehension questions in this text are coded, it is possible for you to determine which kinds of questions give you the most trouble.

On the graph below, keep a record of the questions you have answered incorrectly. Following each selection, darken a square on the graph next to the number of the question missed. The columns are labeled with the selection numbers.

By looking at the chart and noting the number of shaded squares, you should be able to tell which areas of comprehension you are weak in. A large number of shaded squares across from a particular skill signifies an area of reading comprehension weakness. When you discover a particular weakness, give greater attention and time to answering questions of that type.

Further, you might wish to check with your instructor for recommendations of appropriate practice materials.

Categories of Comprehension Skills	Selection																			
	1	2	3	4	5	6	7	8	9	10	11	12	13	14	15	16	17	18	19	20
1. recalling specific facts																				
2. retaining concepts																				
3. organizing facts																				
4. understanding the main idea																				
5. drawing a conclusion																				
6. making a judgment																				
7. making an inference																				
8. recognizing tone																				
9. understanding characters																				
10. appreciating literary forms																				